DUSTY AYRES AND HIS BATTLE BIRDS:
THE BLUE CYCLONE

THE BLUE CYCLONE

By Robert Sidney Bowen

ALTUS PRESS • 2019

CHAPTER 1
BLACK BAIT

S HIVERING, CURLY Brooks tugged the collar of the civilian overcoat tighter about his neck and stared gloomily up the wind-swept, ice-caked street. A fine flurry of snow slithered down, and in the dim light of the street lamps it was like an eerie, mystic shroud descending from heaven.

He shivered again, half turned and glared at Dusty Ayres, also garbed in civilian clothes, pressing back against the building wall to keep clear of the cutting wind.

"Somebody's nuts!" Curly growled. "And I'm damn near frozen stiff!"

Dusty shrugged, banged his gloved hands together.

"Don't boast, sweetheart! I know you're nuts!"

Curly snorted, moved over to him.

"Listen, guy, I've had about enough. Maybe Jack Horner isn't coming."

"Maybe he isn't," Dusty replied. "But I'm still going to wait. I'm curious."

Brooks sighed and slumped against the wall in a gesture of hopeless resignation.

"But what's it all about, Dusty?" he groaned. "We've been waiting over an hour. It's damn near nine!"

"Don't know," was the informing reply. "He simply said for us to meet him here, in civvies."

1

The BLUE CYCLONE
by ROBERT SIDNEY BOWEN

"But for what?" persisted Brooks. "What else did he say? He must have given you some reason! This isn't April Fools' Day!"

Dusty half rolled, shoulder against the wall, to face his pal.

"Listen, little boy!" he bit off. "I've told you everything I know. This afternoon I got a phone call from Jack—from Northeastern Area H.Q. He said for us to meet him here at this corner tonight; to come in civvies, armed, and I said that we would. I started to ask questions, but he cut me off and hung up. Something's in the wind! So I'm going to stick here and find out. You can shove back to the field if you want to!"

Curly gritted his teeth, fished for a cigarette and stuck it between his lips. He glared at Dusty's outstretched hand.

"For that last crack you can smoke one of your own!" he growled. "Of course I'll stick. Someone has to nurse-maid you two! But it all listens screwy to me, that's all. Why the hell couldn't we meet him some place where it's warm? The old think-box can't work so good when I'm cold!"

"Which is the same as in warm weather!" Dusty grunted. "And speaking of warm weather, I'll be damn glad when it comes around. With the Blacks snowed in, nothing has happened for weeks!"

Curly made no comment and both of them lapsed into brooding silence. Each mulled over Dusty's final remark. It was quite true. Winter had settled down with savage earnestness and practically created a mutual cessation of hostilities.

For the last four or five weeks there hadn't been more than a dozen aerial bombing raids by either side. And as for ground troop movements—well, that phase of warfare had come to an absolute standstill. Perhaps winter was not entirely accountable for the last. The Black forces in Canada were not as strong as they had been during the Fall, and it was believed on good authority that Fire-Eyes, supreme commander of the Invaders, and his staff, had gone across the Atlantic to his European stronghold.

Were it any other period of the year, the time would be perfect for a gigantic American offensive all along the Canadian front. But the coming of Winter with its snow, sleet and glare ice, made such a thing a mighty doubtful possibility.

Even the air arm of the Yank forces was held up. Bombing strategic points in good weather was one thing, but bombing them in a blinding snow storm whirling down from the Polar regions was entirely different. It wasn't simply a question of being unable to see their objective—instruments took care of that. It was principally a case of ineffectual results.

The bombing raids didn't tie up mobile troop movements, because no troops were moving. Nor could they pave the way for an American drive. For although the bombs smashed great holes in the ground, even isolated large sectors of Black Invader-occupied territory, they did not remove the miles and miles of chin-deep snow and ice.

Therefore both sides had more or less dug in, and were making plans and preparations for great things when Spring rolled around.

At least, so it seemed. On the other hand, a feeling of tenseness and mystery pervaded the American forces—the aerial branch in particular. Inactivity added to the suspicion that strange chaos was slowly brewing in the hidden background.

In an effort to ferret out the truth, Air Force G.H.Q. had issued standing orders that constant aerial vigilance be maintained. And it had been maintained—but with absolutely no result.

Flying with High Speed Group 7, Dusty had made countless flights, many of them deep into Black territory. But only on two occasions had they met with opposition, and both times had been but a hit-and-miss scrap with a couple of units of Black Darts.

THE ANSWER to it all? Simply the daily increasing feeling that Fire-Eyes intended to strike at some other section of the nation. The history of his conquest of Europe showed that time was the fundamental basis of all his successes.

When weather, or anything else, prevented an onslaught against any given point, he did not waste time waiting for a more favorable opportunity—he simply smashed at some other and more vulnerable point. It was natural that he was planning to do that same thing right now—and the unanswered question in the minds of G.H.Q., and all others who gave it thought, was where and when.

"Extree! Extree! Read all about it! Blacks to sue for peace! Blacks to sue for peace! Extree!"

The shrill cry of a newsboy slipping and sliding along the icy sidewalk jerked Dusty away from his thoughts. He squinted at the lad through the drifting snow, snorted aloud.

"Sue for peace, hell!" he grated. "Editors will print anything for bigger circulation!"

"Yeah!" echoed Curly, rapping bunched fists against each other. "But right now I'd sure love to believe it!"

Faces shielded against the biting wind, they watched the newsboy make a sale to a couple of pedestrians who were interested enough to fish around in the cold for pennies. Presently, the lad cut diagonally across the street and ran up to them.

"Paper, mister? Help me out, will ya? Only got a couple more, and I'm cold."

And as Dusty started to shake his head, "Aw, please, mister! Geez, I need the dough! Me mother—"

"Okay, sonny," Dusty cut him off. "Here's a quarter—keep the paper."

"Nothing doing!" replied the kid, pocketing the coin. "Just take a look at that first page!"

Shoving the paper in Dusty's hand, he yelled, "Thanks, mister!" and went scuttling on down the street shouting his wares.

"Enough profit, and glad to get rid of it, I guess," grunted Dusty, smoothing out the paper.

He stared at the front page. In bold type it contained the headline the newsboy had been shrilling. But it wasn't like headline that caught and held Dusty's eyes. Pinned to the vertical fold was an envelope—a sealed envelope, with no writing on the outside.

"What the hell?" grunted Curly.

Dusty didn't answer. He jerked the pin free, ripped open the envelope, and pulled out the single sheet of paper inside. Together they read the pencil-scrawled message.

> Will pass you in about ten minutes. Take no notice, but watch whoever is trailing me. Follow, and be ready for anything. But do not shoot to kill!
>
> Jack

"Well, I'll be damned!" came from Curly. "More riddles! What do you sup—"

"I don't suppose!" Dusty cut him off, and made as though he were reading the paper. "Got your gun in your pocket ready?"

"Sure!" Curly nodded. "But God knows if I can pull the trigger, what with all ten fingers frozen! So Jack's being trailed, eh? Wonder why he doesn't want us to shoot to kill—in case we have to shoot?"

"Maybe it'll be his mother!" Dusty snapped.

"All right, funny boy!" Curly grated harshly. "Don't tell me another one—my sides are aching!"

Once again they settled into brooding silence. But this time they did not give themselves up to idle thought. On the contrary, they each wracked their brain for some reason that could explain the mysteriousness of Jack Horner, known to a select few as Agent 10, of the U.S. Department of War Intelligence. And at the same time they kept darting sharp glances up and down the street for a first glimpse of their mutual friend.

FIVE MINUTES dragged by, and only two elderly ladies, bodies bent against the wind, went past. Seven minutes, and a group of street urchins went chattering by. Ten minutes and two army officers marched past, neither of whom was Jack Horner in facial appearance, or build for that matter.

Two more minutes and a cop sauntered toward them, stick under his arm, and slapping his obviously numbed hands together. As he drew near, something about his bearing made Dusty stiffen slightly. In the dim glow of the street light, the cop's face was typically Irish—the face of a man too old for military service. Yet, there was something about his carriage— the way he walked—that clicked in Dusty's brain.

As though not even seeing them, the cop came abreast and continued on. But it was at that instant that the words came clearly to them both—whispered words, shot out the corner of the cop's mouth. "Okay, fellows! Eyes open!" It was all Dusty could do not to start forward. He sensed Curly starting at his side, swayed toward him and opened the newspaper.

8

"Hold it, kid!" he hissed. "Don't spoil it now!"

"Don't worry!" came the cryptic reply. "Here, hold the paper down so we can see down the street. Say, isn't that somebody hugging the wall?"

Eyes narrowed, Dusty peered in the direction whence the cop had come. He wasn't sure for a second—and then, suddenly, he saw a shadowy figure close to the wall, about two blocks away. A moment later, as the figure passed within the glow of a street light, he saw the fatigue cap and O.D. great-coat of a U.S. infantry private. He scowled, snapped his eyes around to the back of Agent 10, in cop's uniform, a block to the other side.

"Must be him!" came Curly's voice in his ear. "Can't see anyone but that buck private—and he's sure hugging the building. Wait—he's spotted us, I think! He's moving more out to the curb—walking faster!"

"Yeah!" Dusty grunted. "When he gets within earshot, play up to anything I say."

That took about half a minute. As a matter of fact, the soldier was within twenty yards of the pair when Dusty suddenly folded his paper angrily.

"The hell with those dames, Joe!" he snarled. "We been here an hour. They gave us the run-around!"

"Don't be like that!" Curly clipped back. "I know Bess—I'm telling you she'll show up!"

The soldier was directly opposite them now.

"Sez you!" Dusty grated. "When we're a couple of icicles! I

...DUSTY GOT TO HIS FEET AND CLOSED IN.

ain't waiting half the night for no dame! Come on—let's go 'round to where she works. They both work there, don't they?"

As Dusty spoke he pressed against Curly in a silent signal to wait a moment or two before moving.

"Yeah, they work there, sure!" said Brooks in a loud complaining voice. "But we can't see them until they get out."

"Well I ain't going to wait here another minute!" cried Dusty. "And that's flat! Come on—we're gonna breeze around to her place!"

He started to saunter along behind the soldier, who was now a good half block ahead of them. Over two blocks ahead of the soldier, and almost out of sight in the slithering snow, was Agent 10.

"What a guy, what a guy!" shouted Curly, catching up with Dusty. "All right, we'll go there. Now keep that damn trap of yours shut!"

Then in a soft whisper, "Okay? Shall we close in?"

"No," Dusty murmured back. "Hold it this way. We'll wait for him to do something. Nuts! Like you said—this sure is screwy!"

For six blocks the strange procession continued up the street. Every moment Dusty expected the soldier to turn and glance back. But the man didn't. Hands jammed in the pockets of his great-coat he continued on at an even pace, neither gaining nor losing ground on the dim figure of Agent 10 up ahead.

At the end of the seventh block, Jack Horner turned sharp right and disappeared. Instantly, the soldier quickened his pace;

almost broke into a run, but not quite. Behind him Dusty and Curly put on an equal amount of speed.

For fleeting seconds they lost him as he turned the corner. But, when they turned it, they spotted him again, still the same distance ahead. Jack Horner was considerably closer now, however. To be exact, just one block ahead of the soldier. And he was leading the way down an unlighted street, flanked on both sides by deserted apartment buildings.

For perhaps half a minute everything remained the same. And then, suddenly, the soldier broke into a loping run. His right hand jerked free of his pocket, and although Dusty wasn't sure, he thought that it was clutching something.

However, he didn't stop to figure it out. Jerking his own gun out, he started racing swiftly along the icy sidewalk. Curly Brooks stuck right at his shoulder.

The soldier was within twenty yards of Agent 10, who had not turned, when Dusty saw the man's right hand shoot out, saw the blurred outline of the gas gun clutched in his hand.

"Hold it, you!" he roared.

The sudden and unexpected shout caused the soldier to snap his head around and glance back. At the same instant Dusty's gun crashed out sound. The bullet from it smacked into the pavement at the soldier's feet, ricochetted off and went whining away into the snowy night.

The soldier, still running, darted to one side, drew a bead on Agent 10 with his gas gun. The Intelligence man had dropped flat at Dusty's shout, and now the soldier was almost on top of him.

Dusty was not running when he jerked the trigger again. He was sliding flat-footed over the icy sidewalk. So was Curly Brooks. As a matter of fact, their shots came so close together that they practically blended into one single sound.

A wild cry of pain greeted the echo. The soldier's left leg buckled under him. He tried desperately to regain his balance, but a bullet-shattered leg bone and the icy sidewalk were too much for him. He went sprawling headlong, slid the width of the sidewalk and bumped down over the curb into the snow-filled gutter.

But all the time he clung onto his gas gun, and as he came to a stop he twisted over and swung it around. There was a *pop* and a thin stream of purple smoke spurted out from the tapered muzzle of the gun.

"Lookout!"

Jack Horner's cry of alarm was a waste of breath. Both Dusty and Curly had flung themselves flat, and the deadly stream of gas passed well over their heads to be whipped away by the biting wind.

"Still dumb, eh?" snapped Dusty.

As the words left his lips, he jerked the trigger a third time. Though the light was poor, and the target small, he did not believe in missing. Nor did he miss. The slug from his gun plowed into the soldier's right wrist, and one Black Invader gas gun flew out of numbed fingers and went skating clear across the street to lose itself in a snow-bank.

Ready for more tricks, Dusty got to his feet and closed in. The soldier, however, had had enough for one night. He lay groaning in the snow, nursing his shattered wrist and leg bone. Before Dusty could bend down to inspect the amount of damage. Agent 10 came sliding up, knelt beside the man, and in practically a continuance of the same motion straightened up again.

"Thank God, you didn't kill him!" he breathed heavily.

"You didn't want him that way, did you?" Dusty replied, pocketing his gun. "But what's it all about? And what do we do now?"

"Tell you the first, later," the Intelligence man clipped out. "Right now we take him into the house here. Your shots were probably heard, and there'll be others here in another minute. Certainly timed it perfect—right in front of the house!"

All of which meant little or nothing to either Dusty or Curly. It was Brooks who asked the obvious question.

"What the devil are you raving about?"

Jack Horner hooked his hands under the wounded soldier's armpits.

"Later, I said!" he grunted. "Catch hold—make it snappy! I want to get him out of here!"

Shrugging, the two pilots bent over and took hold of the groaning man. And then with Jack Horner leading the way, they carried him back across the sidewalk and up the front steps of a dark and desolate looking building.

CHAPTER 2
THE MELTING DEATH

ONE OF a bunch of keys that Agent 10 pulled from his pocket opened the heavy front door and admitted them into a pitch-dark hallway. It was only pitch-dark for a second, however. The Intelligence man pocketed the bunch of keys and took out a small flashlight. Its thin beam revealed another door at the end of the hallway. Through this they went, and down a steep flight of stairs to the basement.

At each step the soldier groaned, and whined unintelligible sounds, to which none of the other three paid the slightest attention.

At the bottom of the stairs, young Horner turned left down another hallway toward a third door. They were within a half dozen steps of it, when it swung open and the figure of a middle-aged medical officer was silhouetted against the lighted room behind.

"You're late, lieutenant!" he said, stepping back to make way for them. "I was getting worried!"

Agent 10 made some casual remark that Dusty didn't hear. As a matter of fact, he was too occupied with the appearance of the room into which they had entered. It was like one of several he had seen since his first association with Jack Horner and Intelligence department work.

In other words, the room was fitted out with every communications instrument known to man. Long and short wave radio transmitters and receivers, Cook-ray focusing and recording

16

plates, ground phones, teletype machines, and a dozen other creations of communication science.

Following Jack Horner's lead, Dusty and Curly helped carry the wounded soldier across the room and deposit him in a chair. The instant he let go, the Intelligence man nodded at the medico.

"Nothing much, doc!" he grunted. "Just ease the pain a bit, so that he can concentrate on talking."

And then, twisting back to the soldier, "You are going to talk, you know, Morgan—or whatever the hell your real name is!"

The hiss of an enraged cobra could be no more venomous than the tone of the soldier's voice as he replied through pain-whitened lips.

"You will pay dearly for this, I promise you!"

Agent 10 said nothing, and stepped back to let the medico go to work with the contents of a little brown bag he took from the nearby table. Dusty walked over and faced Horner.

"And now can we play?" he asked. "Or is it still a very deep and dark secret?"

"Check!" Curly echoed. "What's the dope, Jack?"

The Intelligence man didn't answer for the moment. He raised both hands to his face, pulled off strips of make-up clay, pulled wads from his mouth that had given his face its rounded fullness. Presently his face was back to its normal appearance.

"I'm not sure," he said slowly, "that even I know what it's all about. That's why he's here—I'm going to try and find out."

Dusty stared at him, narrowed one eye critically.

"Are we going to play questions and answers?" he grunted. "Or will you tell us what you do know?"

The other sighed, and Dusty could not help but notice the look of utter dejection that fitted across his friend's face.

"There is little to tell," young Horner suddenly got out in a low voice. "A certain trust was placed in me, and—well, I failed. I'm—I'm trying to redeem myself. But I needed the help of you two!"

JACK HORNER

"That goes without saying," said Curly quietly. "What else?"

The Intelligence man seemed to struggle for words. It was as though the full significance of some terrible catastrophe had suddenly descended upon him. His shoulders slumped forward, and a dull, almost listless, look seeped into his ordinarily steel-gray eyes.

Impulsively, Dusty reached out, gripped his arm and squeezed hard.

"We've licked lots of tough things before, kid!" he said in a

GENERAL HORNER

steady voice. "Just give us the facts, so that we all can do a little figuring! What do you say, huh?"

A thin grin twisted Jack Horner's lips.

"Thanks," he said. "Shouldn't be slipping like this—"

He checked himself, and moved over to the far corner of the room, and lowered his voice to little more than a whisper as Curly and Dusty joined him again.

"The Bureau of Chemical Warfare has been working on a secret process known as Metal-Meltic. It's composed of two secret gasses that when mixed create a heat that will melt anything from platinum wire to tempered steel."

"Like those chemical bombs that Ekar used awhile back?" put in Curly.

"Something like them," Agent 10 replied. "Only about ten times more effective. However, I believe the bureau developed the stuff for shell use—long-range use. Alone, neither of the gasses is potent. But when mixed—and they can be mixed by a timing device—the stuff will destroy everything it comes in contact with. A single shell of it will cover a quarter mile area."

"And it's good-bye to every rifle, machine gun, and all other pieces of ordnance, eh?" grunted Dusty.

"Right!" nodded Agent 10. "And, incidentally, a lot of things that are not made of metal. God, by Spring the Black forces up north wouldn't have a gun worth firing, let alone other equipment. But—but now it's gone!"

The last was little more than a moan.

"You mean?" began Dusty. "You mean—"

"That because of me, it's gone. Final tests were to be made a week ago. Made at—well, the place doesn't matter. Major Crandall, chief of the chemical department, was to conduct them. He believed that he was being watched by Black agents. We had him shadowed for a couple of days, but discovered nothing. As an added precaution I was delegated to take the available supply—a single cylinder of each gas—and the formula, to the testing place."

"Good God, the formula, too?" broke in Curly.

"It was necessary for checking during the tests," the other replied. "You see, Major Crandall didn't consider it letter-perfect, as yet. He intended to make further experiments during the tests.

"Anyway, five nights ago, in utmost secrecy, I left Washington by car for the testing place—not more than twenty miles south of here, as a matter of fact.

"Everything was under cover in the back of the car. And on the rear seat rode two armed guards—two of my own men. Nothing happened until we were just outside Hartford, Connecticut. It was close to three A.M., as I remember. And that was the last thing I remember."

The Intelligence man stopped short, made a hopeless gesture with his hands.

"What happened?" Dusty encouraged when the man didn't go on talking.

"I don't know," came the bitter reply. "At least I don't know all the particulars. Everything suddenly became a blank and I passed out cold. When I woke up, it was almost noon. The car was on its side in a ditch, every window, including the windshield, splintered to bits. We'd slammed into a tree.

"I was half in and half out of the car. And my head felt as though it had been split in two. It took me a few minutes to get up onto my feet. Then I saw my two men. They were crumpled up in back—dead!"

THE INTELLIGENCE man stopped short, flicked his eyes across the room to where Morgan was submitting to medical treatment. For a split second young Horner's eyes blazed with a look of savage hate. Then he got control of himself, blinked and looked at Dusty.

"You can guess the rest," he said quietly. "My two men had been gassed. They were in back, of course, and helpless. In some way I must have plowed through one of the windows—that saved me. I found the release spring of a small gas cartridge on the rear floor of the car. Poor devils, they didn't even know what it was they were guarding!"

"But the stuff—the two cylinders, and other things?" broke in Curly.

"It was gone, naturally!" came the bitter answer. "Including the formula I carried in the sole of my boot. Everything gone—and not a single clue!"

"Except?" murmured Dusty. He half nodded toward the man in the uniform of a U.S. infantry private.

"Except him!" Agent 10 replied tight-lipped. "But it took me a couple of days to remember—remember that he was the only possible man who could have known that I was leaving Washington by car with that stuff."

"How'd he know?"

The Intelligence man gestured. "Simple! For a couple of months he's been in charge of our transport division. Fell down on a small job, and the general transferred him to the transport division for punishment. Hell, the same old story—another Black agent practically sleeping with us. God knows how much information he's passed on before this."

"Well, why haven't you nailed him sooner?" frowned Curly.

"For several reasons. One of them, because I wanted to make sure. Not muff it again, and have the real rat get away. And another, because I wanted to make the Blacks start worrying, and thus be able to bait my trap better."

"All of which is as clear as mud," said Dusty. "What the hell would the Blacks have to worry about—assuming, of course, they got the stuff? Which, of course, they did."

"Here's what I mean," Agent 10 replied, speaking rapidly. "According to Crandall, the formula was not entirely complete. He had left out one thing—something to do with generating temperatures, so he said.

"However, he says that expert chemists can, in time, figure that out for themselves, if they have the formula. As for having the two gasses, that doesn't matter. They can not be analyzed, absolutely. It's just a question of discovering the true generating temperatures from the formula. Learning of that—I mean the part left out—gave me what I wanted. The chance to bait my trap."

"Yeah?" queried Curly as the man paused.

"Yeah!" grimly. "So I let it be known—known so that Morgan would be sure to hear—that a new formula had been drawn up—one that included the missing part—and that I was going to communicate it by code to Crandall, at a secret laboratory, tonight.

"To make the thing seem all the more real, Crandall has been in hiding ever since I reported my failure to him. You see—well, I lost the thing—it was all my fault, and, my father, the general, has dumped the job of getting it back into my lap."

Dusty said nothing as Agent 10 stopped talking for a moment. But he knew what was behind the man's words. It was not only a question of duty to country, but one of personal honor as well. General Horner was chief of the department, and his own son the ace operator. But in their work, relationship meant nothing. It was up to Jack Horner to make good. If he didn't—

The Intelligence man was talking again.

"I let Morgan trail me tonight—just long enough to make sure that you two were set. I knew that I could count on you to get him without having to kill him. I didn't dare try it alone—he might have smelled something in the wind."

"You took a hell of a long chance!" grunted Curly Brooks.

"Not so long! Didn't I say that I knew I could count on you two? Anyway, it worked just as I planned it. When he realized that I was coming to this signal station, he started to close in on me. Once I was inside, it would have been too late. And now, by God, he's going to talk—tell me where that stuff was taken, after it was taken from me!"

As the Intelligence man started across the room, Dusty grabbed his arm, pulled him back.

"Wait a minute, kid," he said. "What the hell does it matter whether he talks or not? Crandall knows the formula, doesn't he? What he did once, he can do again."

"No," Jack disagreed. "It's now a race—between our chemical bureau and the Blacks to see who can find the missing generating temperatures first. We've got to see that the Blacks don't win!"

"But Crandall knows!"

"Crandall is dead! He was killed early this morning—shot by some Black rat who smoked him out!"

ROOTED IN his tracks, Dusty dully watched Agent 10 turn and go over to the medico working on Morgan. Then he shook himself out of his trance and quickly joined his Intelligence pal. Curly tagged along at his heels.

"All right, Morgan!" young Horner began in a deadly voice as the medico stepped back from the wounded man. "You know what I want, and I'm giving you a break. The rest of the war in one of our military prisons if you talk, a firing squad if you don't!"

Morgan's lips slid back in a leering grin.

"I don't know what you're talking about, Lieutenant Horner!" he spat out. "But I do know that you'll pay for what's happened tonight!"

The Intelligence man whipped out his hand, grabbed the other's shoulder so tightly that the man groaned aloud.

"Where was the stuff taken? I know damn well that it's still in the country. A snow-flake couldn't have gone through without our knowing it. Speak up, rat! Even you don't want to die!"

The other seemed to half smile, though the features of his face were screwed up in a grimace of pain.

"Threats will do you no good, dog!" he suddenly hissed out. "Kill me, then—kill me! It will get you nothing!"

..DUSTY'S GUN CRASHED FLAME AND SOUND.

Beneath the berserk anger that flushed Agent 10's face, Dusty could see his pal's hopes fading out like a candle flame in a gale of wind. The hope that the man would talk had been a crazy one in the first place. It wouldn't be the first time that a Black agent died with sealed lips. The thing had thrown young Horner off his usual stride. Too much planning, and too few results. Now if only—

"Listen, Jack," he said suddenly. "This bum probably doesn't know anything anyway. And we're wasting time. If I'm going to fly the rest of that stuff for testing, to P Fourteen tonight, I've got to be on my way. We'll just hand this guy over to a firing squad and forget him! That'll be just one less of them for us to worry about!"

Agent 10's eyes widened.

"Huh? You fly to P Fourteen? Why—"

"Pipe down!" Dusty cut him off hastily. "I didn't mean to— wait a minute! Is there some other place where we can talk?"

Jack Horner, eyes still wide and brows furrowed in a puzzled frown, jerked a thumb toward a second door leading off from the room.

"There's a bunk-room in there," he said.

"Then we'll go in there," said Dusty. "You too, doc!"

As he spoke, the pilot walked over to the door through which they had first entered, twisted the key in the lock, and dropped the key in his pocket. Then he motioned Agent 10, Curly Brooks and the medico toward the other door.

"The tramp will be here when we want him," he said. "Come

on, make it snappy. I want to outline something to the three of you, before I leave."

"Listen—"

"Listen, nothing!" Dusty snapped off Agent 10's outburst. "Into the bunk-room, will you?"

The Intelligence man hesitated a split second, then with a muttered curse, led the way into the bunk-room, snapping on the light as he entered. As soon as they were all in, and the door had been shut, he whirled on Dusty.

"Now, for God's—"

Dusty clapped a hand over his mouth.

"Shut up!" he breathed fiercely. "All of you, shut up! Let's play it my way for a couple of moments. I've a hunch we'll learn a lot more than by just sailing into him. Hell, you can't make that type talk unless they don't realize it!"

Agent 10 gritted his teeth but said nothing. Like Curly and the medico, he stood looking at Dusty in befuddled anger. The ace pilot, however, ignored them, slid softly up to the door, pressed his ear against it.

For five solid minutes he didn't move, even when Curly impatiently plucked him on the sleeve. Finally, though, he straightened up, flashed them a grin.

"Okay," he grunted. "I think he's taken in hook, line and sinker."

"Damn you, Ayres!" grated young Horner. "What the hell's this all about?"

"That's what I'm going to find out," Dusty grunted, and jerked open the door.

MORGAN, OR whatever his true name might be, was slumped down in the chair. He didn't even look up as Dusty and the others re-entered the room. Giving him but a sidelong glance, Dusty continued on past him to the rear wall covered with communication instruments. He stopped and stared at them a moment, then turned back and grinned at the others.

"The old hunches are still working for me!" he said. "And the latest has worked perfect!"

Agent 10 cursed, reached him in two bounding steps.

"Out with it!" he shouted. "Out with it!"

For an answer Dusty pointed his finger at the outgoing message recorder of the high-speed wireless unit. Agent 10 took a good look and gasped aloud.

"Hell! A message was sent out on this four minutes ago!"

"Right!" Dusty grunted, moving over in front of the fake infantryman. "I heard our boy friend, here, trying to muffle the key. I saw you looking at the set, rat, and it gave me ideas!"

The Black looked at him with scornful eyes.

"Clever! But you only fooled yourself. You forget that the recorder does not record the nature of the message being sent!"

Dusty laughed at the words.

"One for you, sweetheart!" he snapped. "But I knew what the message would be, you see. And your rat friends waiting for me at P Fourteen will be in for a nice little surprise!"

The soldier started violently, tried to cover it up by shifting his position on the chair.

Jack Horner, most of his scowl gone, came over to Dusty.

"We all seem to be acting riddles, tonight," he said. "What's the right answer?"

Dusty shrugged.

"Simple enough. Saw this rat eyeing the wireless unit when I spoke about flying some stuff to P Fourteen. 'Stuff' meant either the real formula or some more Metal-Meltic, to him. So when I gave him the chance to get at the set, he took it and sent out the news."

"But we don't know where he sent it!" Curly Brooks blurted out.

"Right!" echoed Jack Horner.

Dusty gave them both a look of annoyance.

"Who cares?" he grated. "Don't you get the point? There'll be company waiting for me at P Fourteen—that old deserted airdrome just north of Oil City, Pennsylvania, in case you don't know it. Can you get a couple of cylinders, Jack? Like, the ones the stuff is carried in? Get them right away?"

"Sure! But—"

"Swell! Now listen, I'm going to drop the stuff by flare chute. Have some of your trusted men covering the place but don't let them run out and pick it up. Wait for the Black agents, who are bound to be there, to get it. Then tail them to wherever they go.

"If the real stuff is still in the country, they'll lead you to wherever it is.

"As an extra precaution, Curly and Biff Bolton will tail me in the air—and we'll take up the chase, in case they use a hidden plane. If it does work that way, be sure that Intelligence H.Q.

is tuned in on my wave-length all the time. But do not under any circumstances try to talk with me, unless I talk first. Got it?"

Jack Horner nodded. "God, it may work out that way, at that!" he breathed.

"Sure it will!" Dusty came right back. "Now let's get going."

As he talked he turned his back on the Black agent, and started herding the others toward the door.

"Wait—look out! He's—"

Dusty whirled, right hand streaking for his holstered service automatic. The fake soldier had thrown himself from his chair, twisted in mid-air, and was now clawing with his good hand for the wireless key. He had reached it, and clicked out perhaps two letters, when Dusty's gun spat flame. Not a sound came from the man's lips. His body was slammed up against the instrument-covered wall by force of the bullet that caught him square between the shoulder blades. Then he slowly fell over on his right side and slumped down onto the floor, stone dead.

Dusty holstered his gun without giving the dead Black spy a second look. "Now, I know my guesses were right!" he said under his breath. "I was hoping the rat would make a break for the key. Come on—now we go to work!"

CHAPTER 3
THE BLUE CYCLONE

"A LL RIGHT, you two. Tag me as far behind as you
can without losing my tail running light, see? And
keep your eyes peeled for any plane that may take off. O.K.?"

Dusty toed out his cigarette on the snow-crusted tarmac,
and gave Curly and Biff Bolton a keen look. They both nodded,
but it was Curly who spoke.

"That'll be easy enough," he said, "tailing your running lights.
But suppose the hidden plane they may use isn't near the field?
I mean—they'll use the plane later, when they get to it by car."

"That's taken care of," Dusty nodded. "Jack has a portable
radio-sending set. Once I drop the empty cylinders, I'm to circle
around—every circle bigger and bigger, but keeping in his
sending area. If they do what you say, Jack will let me know at
once. You'll know too. Then it will be up to us to pick up the
ship and stick with it. Any more questions? Time to go."

"Not that it's important," rumbled Biff Bolton, "but how
come you're taking the Flash instead of your X-Diesel?"

Dusty looked at the Silver Flash IV setting with prop idling
over on the tarmac in front of the end hangar. He shrugged,
smiled faintly.

"For no particular reason," he murmured. "Nothing, except
that it happens to be just a year ago today that I set that world's
speed record in the first Flash. Just figure I'll use her—sort of
an anniversary flight, you know."

Jumping quickly to the side to miss Dusty's booted foot

coming up, Curly saluted with the usual raspberry and ran over to his own plane. Biff Bolton hung back, just long enough to give Dusty an odd look.

"Know *just* how you feel, skipper," he mumbled. "Planes are just like human beings to me, too. Curly—I just guess he never will take things like that seriously."

"I hope not," Dusty laughed. "Two old sentimental gray-beards like you and I are enough for one unit. See you aloft, pronto."

As Dusty walked over and climbed into the Flash IV a warm look seeped into his eyes and for a moment he hesitated in releasing the wheel brakes, and opening the throttle, to enjoy that inexpressible something that surges through a pilot who, after a long absence, once more returns to fly an old familiar plane. The feeling, if words can express it, is akin to a reunion of tried and true pals.

A moment or two later, though, thoughts of the job to be done took charge of him, and with face grim he taxied out onto the field, slued the ship around on its ski-wheel landing gear and went streaking up into the air. The fine flurry of snow had long since spent itself, and a stiff wind had whipped the low-hanging clouds elsewhere, leaving in their place a limitless canopy of winking stars.

Holding the nose up toward them, Dusty snapped on the single tail running light, sealed the cockpit hood, and set his radio dial for transmitting and receiving on his own personal wave-length. That accomplished, he ruddered around until he was on a crow's course for P Fourteen, then snapped off the dash light.

Tearing upward and forward through the dark air seemed to steady his thoughts regarding the job ahead. Not only did it steady them, but also filled him with a certain unflinching confidence that it would be a cinch.

Poor old Jack! The thing had certainly smacked him square between the eyes. He was taking it as a great gob of muck splashed against a perfect record sheet. Hell, he must get the stuff back, and snap Jack out of his dizzy way of taking things.

The sudden blinking of the red signal light on the radio panel put an end to Dusty's ruminations. For a split second he wondered why no words crackled out of the ear-phones. Then he realized that the signals were not on his wave-length. They were on a band close enough to his to make the red light blink. Impulsively, he reached out his free hand and gingerly turned the dial knob. The result meant very little, however. True, he got sound. But it was a fuzzy sound.

"Not static-jamming!" he grunted aloud. "So what the hell?"

Concentrating on the dial knob and volume rheostat, he fiddled with both for a couple of minutes. But to no avail. He succeeded only in making the fuzzy sound louder in tone. Yet, he could tell that some voice was broadcasting. Several times the ear-phones crackled out distinct individual syllables. Not enough, though, to convey any meaning to him.

AND THEN like a smack between the eyes the truth came to him. The station broadcasting had a failing generator. It could only raise enough power to make separated signals clear. Between the clear signals the power would fail and the signals become just fuzzy sound—something like the drone of a bee on a hot summer's day.

Snapping on the dash light, he squinted at the station direction finder. The needle on the dial was quivering back and forth. It was as though the instrument were human and reluctant to make up its mind. Accurate recording was impossible. He could only make several guesses as to what the true reading might be, and then strike an average. That average, however, jerked him up straight in the seat with a startled grunt. It placed the sending station somewhere in the P Fourteen area—the very spot for which he was headed!

"I must be wrong!" he muttered aloud. "For one thing, there isn't any known station located there. And Jack and his men couldn't possibly have reached there, yet. Why, it—"

The sudden thought came to him like a bolt of lightning.

"Unless the Blacks are there with a portable set of their own!" he exclaimed. "A portable set that's going haywire on them!"

For a moment or two he mulled it over, reached a grim decision and twisted the wave-length dial back to his own reading.

"Calling Jocko, calling Jocko!" he droned into the transmitter tube. "What big eyes you have, grandma! All the better to see with, my dear. Yes, grandma, we must always look before we leap. Yes, my dear, now turn on the radio and let's see what we can hear."

Slapping the transmitter tube back on its hook, he stared flint-eyed out into the dark night, and waited—hoping against hope. Hoping that Jack Horner had picked up his crazy message and realized that it was a warning for him to watch his step, and that strange signals were streaking through the night skies.

For ten minutes or more, he sat as man of stone expecting to hear some answering signal from Jack, far down there on the ground. But none came through, and a worried scowl lined his forehead. Why didn't young Horner send him some sort of an answering signal? He must have received his message. Hadn't they arranged to keep all sets on the same wave-length?

The red signal light blinked at last! But the voice that crackled out of the earphones was like a bombshell from out of nowhere.

"Change your course to due north, Captain Ayres!"

Struck dumb for the moment, Dusty could only gape wide-eyed in the darkness. Suddenly the voice spoke again.

"I'm on your wave-length, Captain Ayres! Change your course to due north!"

"Who the hell are you?"

Dusty blurted out the words almost before he realized that he had spoken them. The unknown voice had been quite clear and moderate in tone. As a matter of fact it was like the voice of a cultured American. Then it spoke for the third time.

"I have no time for questions, Captain Ayres! I am simply giving you orders. Change your course to due north—and keep it until ordered otherwise!"

The Yank pilot cursed softly, unconsciously balled his free fist. It wasn't a Black Invader voice, that was certain—no harshness or grating tone to it. So what American was trying to tell him where to head in?

"Whoever you are!" he thundered into the transmitter tube, "get the hell on your way! I've got other things to do!"

"Quite true," came back the instant reply. "You are on your way to drop something quite valuable, at a certain destination. But you are not going to do it, captain. You're going to do what I tell you to do!"

As the words came to him, Dusty immediately changed his original opinion. The unknown speaker couldn't possibly be a Yank. All those who knew of his mission would never communicate with him—until he gave the signal. True, he'd given that signal to Agent 10. But this was not Jack Horner's voice. As far as he knew, he had never heard it before in his life.

Leaning forward, and snapping off the dash light, he squinted up into the night skies. He had already taken a flash glance at the station direction finder and found that the mysterious broadcaster was located within a quarter of a mile of his own position. Perhaps more, perhaps less. That didn't matter. He knew that the broadcaster was close to him. And what's more— in the air!

But as he peered at the canopy of stars, he could see no telltale shadow streaking across their twinkling brilliance. Even when he slipped around in a dime turn and studied the heavens in back of him, he still saw nothing.

"There's a ship close to me!" he grunted aloud. "I know damn well there is!"

The mysterious voice speaking again made him realize that his radio set was still open.

"Of course there is, captain! I am very close to you! And telling you for the last time—change your course to due north!"

Dusty was on the point of telling the unknown just what he could do, and to where he could go. But he suddenly changed his mind, and grabbed up the transmitter tube.

"Hey, string bean!" he barked. "Mama goes where papa goes!"

Those words off his tongue he banked the Flash around toward the north and flew steadily forward.

"Counting on you, Curly," he whispered to himself. "He's spotted me because of my running light. You follow it too, and maybe between the three of us we'll—"

"Captain Ayres!" the unknown voice cut in. "Your quaint remark was undoubtedly a signal to others. If you value your life and theirs, I would most sincerely suggest that you tell them to go elsewhere."

THE LAST jolted Dusty into the firm belief that the mysterious broadcaster had guessed the true meaning of his signal to Curly. In fact, there was no doubt that he had. For a moment or two he glared hard at the radio panel, trying desperately to decide on his next move. If the unknown was a Black—and hell, he must be—why didn't he attack him? The answer to that was one of two things—either the bum was too yellow to take chances or he believed that the Flash carried cylinders of Metal-Meltic, or the complete formula.

Dusty suddenly smashed his free fist against the side of the cockpit.

"That's it!" he breathed fiercely. "The tramp wants this stuff. And he doesn't dare crack me down—or try to—for fear it will destroy itself. Yeah, it must be that."

A plan of action leaping into his brain, he grabbed up the transmitter tube.

"Bean pole!" he snapped. "Amscray with the boy friend. Them's orders! Never mind the check-back! Git!

Snapping off the set, he gave the Flash its head, and sat staring straight out into the darkness. Tingling ripples of suppressed excitement raced up and down his spine. The whole thing was working out far better this way. Instead of trying to trail the Black to the secret hiding place—if there was one—he was letting the Black escort him there.

True, everything wasn't entirely clear. Who was this unknown who gave him orders? What kind of a ship was he flying? And just where was he, right now? There was no answer for either of the three questions. However, they would undoubtedly be answered later.

The important item was, that to all appearances, the Blacks had not as yet figured out the missing generating temperatures. Else, why come after him?

Good! In fact, swell! Things were working out for a perfect chance to breeze right into the enemy's camp. So long as they continued to believe that he had Metal-Meltic with him, his skin was as safe as could be. Once they found out the truth—hell, plenty of time to figure on that later.

The blinking of the red signal light cut in on his jumbled thoughts. He flipped up the contact switch and spun the wave-length dial knob, half guessing the voice he would hear. His half guess was correct. The unknown Black spoke in the earphones.

"Throttle your engine and go into a glide, captain. Keep your glide toward the north. We'll land in a few moments!"

The words were like a dash of icy water over Dusty's hopes. Land in a few moments? A quick glance at the roller map brought a groan to his lips. His position was just a few miles south of Rochester, New York. A glide would take him down onto the old 207th Infantry camp, just this side of the city. No chance of there being any hiding place of the Blacks in that section of ground. The answer? Simple! Yeah, simple as hell!

The unknown, riding herd on him, was going to force him to land, relieve him of his "precious" cargo, and then carry on by himself. Carry on, after jerking a gun trigger a couple of times, perhaps!

"Wrong again, Dusty!" he grated softly. "The tramp isn't as dumb as you thought he was."

Eyes agate, lips pressed together in a thin line, he reached out and pulled back on the throttle and sent the Flash coasting down toward the ground.

For three minutes he held the plane in the glide, all the while half turned in the seat and peering hard up toward the stars. Then suddenly, his lips curled back in a tight grin.

For the fleeting part of a second he saw the blurred shadow sliding down, about three thousand feet above him. Just a blurred shadow that was gone almost instantly.

But it gained him the advantage that he desired. And in one

sweeping motion of his free hand, he snapped off the dash light, and the tail running light, and banged the throttle wide open. A split second later he hauled the stick back into his stomach, and sent the Flash arcing up in the first half of a gigantic loop.

Almost instantly, the unknown voice spoke in the ear-phones.

"You are a fool, captain! You force me to kill you!"

Upside-down, head thrown back, Dusty stared down at the streaking silhouette of a barrel-fuselaged monoplane pursuit. In the darkness, it was impossible to spot details. But he didn't bother about that. He didn't have too. His surprise maneuver had reversed everything. Now he was top man. And his thumbs were itching to jab home the electric trigger trips.

"Thanks for the tip!" he snapped into the transmitter tube. "But now it's your time to dance."

"You fool, I repeat! You are forcing me to kill you! And for the present, I have no such desire. Land as I ordered you to."

"Listen, big shot!" Dusty countered, "maybe this will put a bit of common sense into your thick skull!"

As he spoke, he jabbed home the right gun trigger trip, and set a hissing shower of hot steel slithering down through the left wing of the plane below.

"Next time, it will be a hell of a sight closer!" he thundered. "Now—"

"Very well, fool, if you insist!"

THE WORDS crackling out of the earphones were immediately followed by a weird sky phenomenon that chilled Dusty to the marrow of his bones.

As though by magic a hazy, wavy ribbon of blue fire cut a

path through the inky air. Grotesquely it curved up toward him, changing inky darkness into a shimmering conglomeration of blue shades. For split seconds every muscle in his body seemed paralyzed. Even his brain refused to function. Like a man of stone he sat gaping at the weird scene in the night sky.

And then, suddenly, he was conscious of his voice bellowing out in wild alarm; conscious that he was whipping the Flash around on wing-tip and striving desperately to zoom up away from the wavy ribbon of blue fire that was reaching out for him in the night.

And also, he became conscious of the cool voice of the unknown pilot speaking in the ear-phones—speaking as though he were making casual mention of some unimportant incident.

"Rather an interesting sight, eh, captain? But you have only yourself to blame, you know. I gave you your chance—but you force me to extreme measures. Goodbye, Captain Ayres. I am truly sorry that it should turn out this way. I had wished to meet you face to face, in person. Goodbye, Captain Ayres!"

Words—words that seemed to come from a million miles away and beat against Dusty's brain with triphammer effect. Everything was spinning around in a blue haze. A terrific heat was seemingly searing every square inch of his body.

He felt as though he were literally on fire. Automatically, he hurled and tossed his plane around in a berserk effort to get clear of the sea of blue fire that seemed to curve up at the edges and engulf him.

One instant he was tearing around on wing-tip. The next he

was zooming full out toward the stars. And the next he was thundering down toward the ground.

Suddenly something seemed to let go in his head with a terrific explosion. It was the radio tubes blowing out in the terrific heat. But he didn't know it. As a matter of fact, he had suddenly gone numb to everything. Movement of the stick and rudder pedals was instinctive. Flying instinct was keeping him in the air. That and nothing else.

A blue shimmering haze, weaving a cockeyed crazy pattern in the sky. A blue, shimmering haze that seemed to actually give off a sort of roaring hissing sound. A blue cyclone engulfing the Flash, the stars, everything, in its swirling vortex. And he was going down; slipping, sliding, spinning down into a roaring and crackling blue hell. For one infinitesimal period of time his brain was released from its paralytic spell long enough to grasp that fact.

Spinning, whirling down toward earth! Helpless to move a single muscle, he was caught fast in the whirling maelstrom of blue hell! Down—down—down—

CHAPTER 4
VANISHED BUZZARD

EYES RED-RIMMED, face gaunt and haggard, Curly Brooks paced up and down the length of the mess lounge, puffing furiously on a cigarette. Slouched in a nearby chair, chin cupped in his big hands, sat Biff Bolton. In another chair sat Major Drake, C.O. of High Speed Group No. Seven. Save for

Curly's feet thumping against the floor, there wasn't a single sound. The very air of the room seemed charged with electrified silence.

Presently, Curly broke it as he cursed savagely and hurled his half-smoked cigarette into the fireplace.

"If I only knew where he was!" he intoned. "Only knew that he was alive! Good God, I'm going mad doing nothing!"

For emphasis he smashed one clenched fist against the palm of the other hand.

"I'll go mad, I tell you!" he repeated in a wild tone. "Stark, raving mad! Dusty—the swellest man God ever made! Gone—gone, God knows where!"

He shrugged hopelessly and resumed his restless pacing.

"Sit down, son," said Major Drake quietly. "You're just wearing yourself out. Sit down and tell me the whole thing again. Maybe you forgot something."

Curly smiled wryly, dropped into a chair.

"Didn't forget anything," he mumbled. "There wasn't anything to forget. Just before we would have reached the P Fourteen area, someone cut in on Dusty's wave-length—started ordering him north, like I said. He also knew what Dusty was up to. Dusty gave me the tip to tag along, but this rat, whoever he is, got wise. So Dusty told us two to beat it."

"But didn't you spot this ship—this other ship?" Major Drake asked.

Curly looked at Biff, and they both shook their heads.

"No," Brooks said. "At least, not up to that time. We could

see Dusty, of course—he had on his tail running light, but later—"

He stopped, looked at Bolton again.

"What was your impression, Biff?"

"Don't know how to put it," mumbled the big pilot, scowling heavily. "I saw the skipper's tail light go out—heard this other guy calling him a fool and so forth. And then—well, it was sort of like a smoke screen on fire. Only it was blue flames instead of red. Wavy like—sort of transparent, too. Of course we were pretty far behind, but I spotted the shipper's ship. He was trying like hell to get away from the stuff. Hadn't touched him yet. And—"

"And it was then that I saw the other crate!" cut in Curly. "Saw it in the reflection of the blue stuff. It was a radial Diesel pursuit monoplane. A big job, though. An all-red ship, I think. It—"

"And the blue stuff was coming back off the top of the rudder post!" added Biff. "Just like a sky-writing ship, if you know what I mean."

Major Drake nodded.

"Guess I get the idea," he said. "And then—then, what happened?"

Curly gritted his teeth, bunched his fists.

"We lost sight of Dusty. The stuff got between him and us. I think he went down in a spin. I'm not sure, though. He was still a couple of miles away. About the same time we lost the other crate, too. It stopped spitting out the blue fire, and just seemed to fade into the night.

"When we reached the place the blue stuff had faded out. We circled, and tried to get Dusty on the radio—but didn't get a thing."

"We even went down and dropped flares on the snow!" spoke up Biff. "Hunted for him in case he crashed. But—"

The big pilot's sad gesture finished the sentence. For a couple of moments silence settled over the room again. Presently, Major Drake made a snapping sound with his lips.

"He'll show up!" he said with a conviction none of them felt. "We'll be hearing from him soon. He was always a fool for luck, you know. I have a feeling that it won't fail him, this time."

Curly said nothing. He glanced at his watch and saw that it was close to noon. A little under twelve hours since he'd last seen his closest pal. He twisted his wrist so that Major Drake could see the watch.

"Twelve hours, and no word!" He said desperately. "If he was okay, we would have heard by now. Dammit, I can't stand this waiting. I'm going looking for him."

"You're going to park right here!" Major Drake barked. And then in a softer tone. "Be sensible Brooks! You haven't the faintest idea where to start looking."

"Maybe he crashed near Rochester! I could look there, and see if—"

"That area is now being gone over with a fine-tooth comb," the C.O. cut in patiently. "If he's crashed, he'll be found. And you forget the message that came through from Lieutenant Horner a couple of hours ago. He's on his way here now and he distinctly requested that you two wait for him. Perhaps he'll have news."

AT THAT moment the roar of twin engines came to their ears. Rushing over to the nearest window they stared up into the slate-colored winter sky. A twin-engined cabin ship was streaking down toward the field. No sooner had it landed than the cabin door opened and Jack Horner jumped down onto the ground. Breaking into a run he came over to the mess, in through the door. Curly grabbed him.

"Jack! You've heard from him?"

The Intelligence man frowned, shook his head.

"Not a word," he said sadly. "Not a word since you contacted me this morning and said that he was missing. Damn, if I could only have gotten through to him last night. If that blasted set of mine hadn't gone screwy!"

"Then that was you?" cried Biff Bolton. "That was your set making that fuzzy sound?"

"Yes! We reached the place ahead of time. Found that the Two-seventy-eight motorized gun outfit was there. Dusty didn't know when he selected that place. I tried to tell him by radio. Naturally, the Two-seventy-eight being there knocked Dusty's original plan into a cocked hat, at least from the ground angle. I wanted to tell him that so that he'd concentrate on the air end entirely. But I couldn't get through—couldn't even hear a message that he tried to send me."

Agent 10 stopped talking, stared thoughtfully at the floor. Curly stood it as long as he could.

"But—but what's the plan?" he asked sharply. "Why did you

want us to wait here for you? Good God, maybe by now Dusty's—"

"Steady, Brooks!" the C.O. slipped out. "Give Lieutenant Horner a chance to talk. You have an angle on the thing, lieutenant?"

"Maybe and maybe not," was the noncommittal reply. "If what you say about that blue stuff is true—the Black who flew that ship is the Black who got those two cylinders of Metal-Meltic from me!"

The announcement was like a bombshell going off in the room. Curly peered hard at the man.

"You mean—"

"I mean that Metal-Meltic is wavy blue in appearance," the Intelligence man broke in. "I mean that the Blacks are using the stuff for air work—what they have of it."

"God!" choked out Major Drake. "Then if Ayres was caught by it—"

"There'd be nothing left of him, or his ship," Agent 10 said in a hushed voice. "If it caught him, Dusty's—Dusty's gone!"

Curly sank into a chair with a bitter groan of dejected misery. But he was up on his feet again almost instantly.

"No!" he said fiercely. "It didn't work out that way! It just couldn't! It isn't in the cards for Dusty to go—like that! I feel it—feel it, here!"

As he spoke the last he thumped his right clenched fist against his chest. Then suddenly he gave Agent 10 a queer look.

"There's something else on your mind!" he said almost harshly. "Let's have it."

The Intelligence man pursed his lips, sucked in air with a whistling sound.

"No matter what's happened to Dusty," he said slowly, "he'd want us to carry on with the job of getting the stuff back. Or at least preventing the Blacks from using it. It may sound crazy, but I think that the formula and the stolen Metal-Meltic are in the country."

"What, lieutenant?" Major Drake shot at him. "What makes you think that it hasn't been flown into Black territory?"

"Because, sir," replied young Horner, "if it had been taken out, I'd know about it."

"Meaning what?" grunted Curly as the other paused.

"Anything so important as that would create quite a stir back of the Black lines. Our agents there would be bound to hear about it, and would communicate with us at once.

"But for the last week, their reports have contained no news of any interest, simply plain reports of increasing inactivity in Black territory. And another reason that makes me believe it's still within our borders is a report that came through to me early this morning. It is an unconfirmed report that there are Blacks in the Rocky Mountains!"

"The Rocky Mountains?" boomed Major Drake. "Where— where in them?"

"I don't know," was the reply. "But the report—from a trusted agent incidentally—states of the sighting of Black Invader planes over the western part of Montana, near the Butte, Helena and Virginia City areas. As you know, you could hide half a hundred army corps in the region, and nobody would be the wiser."

"Granted," nodded the C.O. "But planes sighted over the mountain regions don't necessarily mean that there are Blacks in the mountains!"

"Of course not, sir," replied Agent 10, a trifle tartly. "I am quite aware of that.

"But try and look at it this way. What's the idea of Blacks patrolling those mountainous regions? To bomb them? For what gain? None, absolutely! As regard inflicting damage on us, they might just as well bomb the middle of the Atlantic.

"True the cities of Butte, Helena and Virginia City offer something in the way of objectives. But if my reports are correct, none of the planes sighted came anywhere near the cities.

"And it so happens that no enemy planes have been sighted, or spotted by ground detectors, either coming or going over the Canadian line. Further, none has been spotted, or heard, crossing any of the borders of Montana!"

Major Drake seemed unimpressed. His next words proved it beyond doubt.

"The last," he said, "is perhaps because they crossed at high altitude. And as for the first—I repeat, planes in the air do not necessarily mean troops on the ground."

"Troops, no," Agent 10 reasoned patiently. "But let us say that Blacks are establishing a H.Q. base for Intelligence activities within our borders. That is possible, also practical, you must admit."

"I do," grudgingly. "But I'm still unconvinced that both the formula and the stolen supply of Metal-Meltic have not been taken out of the country. Hell, on the face of it, it follows that they'd get it to their own laboratories as fast as they could. But that brings a question to mind. I understand that Crandall, the inventor of the stuff, was killed. Did he make out a new and complete formula before he died?"

Jack Horner sighed, stared gloomily at the opposite wall.

"Not that we know of," he said. "At least he did not turn it over to the Bureau of Chemical Warfare. He was to have done that yesterday. Frankly, the thing was such a close secret with him that he made no record at all of the correct generating temperatures. While he was in hiding he planned to work them out, and then give them to the bureau."

"So," grunted the C.O., "it's up to the bureau to figure them out without his assistance? In other words, the bureau and the Blacks are more or less starting from scratch? They have an equal opportunity to profit from American genius, eh?"

"Unless we can do something about it, yes!" nodded Agent 10 heavily.

"To hell with that!" Curly Brooks blurted out. "That can wait! My first job is to find Dusty!"

"Check!" rumbled Biff Bolton. "And I'm gonna do it, even if I have to slug every Black rat still alive!"

Jack Horner gave them both a bitter look.

"Don't you suppose I feel the same way?" he grated. "If it hadn't been for my blunder, my damn foolishness, he'd be with us now! If you think—"

Curly leaned forward, took hold of his arm.

BIFF BOLTON

"Steady, Jack!" he said quietly. "We'll be smacking each other in a moment—and for nothing. We're all in the same boat. We want to learn the truth about Dusty. Find out if he's—we want to find him."

"Sorry," the Intelligence man grinned. "Guess I spoke out of turn. Yes, yes, of course we all want to find out about Dusty. No news of his plane? It hasn't been found, yet?"

Curly shook his head.

"Not yet. But, if that stuff got him, we might never find what—was left!"

Brooks suddenly spun toward the C.O.

"I'm sorry, sir," he got out rapidly, "but I've stuck here long enough. I've got to join in the hunt. I've got to do something! Even if it's only flying over where we last saw him. I'm not going to stick around here any longer!"

THE C.O. said nothing. Simply looked at Curly, and at Biff waiting at Curly's shoulder. Then he started to speak, but only succeeded in opening his mouth when the radio signal buzzer on the desk cut him off short. He whirled toward the small set, and flipped up the switch.

"Drake on Seven-two-four!" he barked. "Go ahead!"

The tiny built-in speaker crackled and hummed a bit, and then gave forth words.

"Niagara Base H.G. calling! The plane described as belonging to Captain Ayres has been found."

"Found? Found?" echoed the C.O. in a loud voice. "When? Where was it found? How is the pilot? How is Captain Ayers?"

"Please do not interrupt until the message is completed!" crackled the voice in the speaker unit. "The plane, known as the Silver Flash, was found ten minutes ago in a field just north of Batavia.

"It is undamaged save for some scorch marks on the right lower wing. The pilot was not found. A search is being made for him now, in the event he left the plane by parachute. But according to the radioed report from the searching party that

54

found the plane, it is not believed that Captain Ayres left the plane by parachute."

"Why?" Major Drake thundered into the transmitter tube. "What do you mean by that? Why not?"

The speaker unit gave forth sounds that were very much akin to cursing. Then came the words.

"There are no bullet holes in any part of the plane. And it seems to be in perfect mechanical order. The glass of the alcohol compass is broken and there are blood stains on the metal rim and on the cockpit floorboards. It indicates that the pilot was thrown forward when landing, and struck his head on the compass."

"But he can't be far away!" the C.O. shot back. "And he must have left a trail in the snow! What about tracks?"

"There are tracks," came the reply. "But they are tracks of another plane landing, and taking off. Also footprints going from the plane tracks over to the captain's plane and back again. They are almost obliterated though—as if something had been dragged over them!"

"Such as Captain Ayres' body?" barked Major Drake.

"Perhaps. What do you wish us to do? Shall we move the plane?"

Curly leaped forward and practically snatched the transmitter tube from out of the C.O.'s hand.

"Leave everything as it is!" he roared. "Don't let anyone touch a damn thing! We're on our way up there now. Don't let anyone touch a damn thing, understand?"

"I understand," replied the voice in the earphones stiffly. "Signing off!"

Curly didn't hear the last. He had thrust the transmitter tube back into Major Drake's hand and was bounding toward the door.

"Biff!" he bellowed over his shoulder. "Shake it up! This is a start for us, anyway!"

"A start for all of us!" roared Major Drake, grabbing Jack Horner's arm and pulling him along. "We'll all go in your cabin job!"

CHAPTER 5
ONE-MAN PATROL

"I KNEW he couldn't go out that way! I just knew it! It wasn't in the cards! He's still alive!"

Curly roared out the words with forced joy, as he pulled the twin engined cabin job off the crusted snow and poked its nose toward the western Massachusetts skies.

"A miracle, if there ever was one!" echoed Major Drake, in back with Biff Bolton and Jack Horner. "But, good God, why didn't they find him when they found the plane. Hitting the compass knocked him out—but he couldn't have gone far away."

"Unless, maybe he was kidnaped, huh?" Biff put in.

The C.O. shrugged, sat scowling at the back of Curly's neck.

"From that angle, it doesn't make sense," he said dubiously. "To all intents a very definite effort was made to kill him. By a miracle he escaped, got down on the ground, and cracked his skull. Let us say that the other pilot followed him down to get the stuff he was believed to be carrying. All right! Why take Ayres along, too?"

"If the Black Hawk, or Ekar, were alive, I could answer that one," Curly grunted back over his shoulder. "But say Jack—would you swear that stuff we saw was Metal-Meltic?"

No answer from the Intelligence man caused Curly to turn around in the seat and look straight at him. Young Horner was slumped down in his seat, gazing through half closed eyes out the side cabin window. He seemed totally oblivious to all that was going on inside the cabin.

"Hey Jack!" Brooks shouted. "Still think that stuff was Metal-Meltic? Maybe—"

The Intelligence man kept his eyes fixed on the air outside and slowly shook his head.

"I don't know what to think, yet!" he muttered. "If Dusty didn't go through the stuff, it could still have been Metal-Meltic. But if he did go through it, and only got a scorched wing, it's a cinch it wasn't Metal-Meltic. I'm thinking more about the kidnap angle than of how he escaped."

"And what are you thinking about it?" Major Drake shot at him. "Got any ideas?"

With tantalizing effect, young Horner shook his head again.

"Nothing worth mentioning at the moment."

The others grunted, and heavy silence settled over the group. Up forward in the pilot's seat, Curly held the ship on a crow course for Batavia, New York. He hadn't bothered about altitude; speed being the essential thing. And now, with automatic movements he kept the craft on even keel, skimming across the peaks of the Berkshire Mountains and west over the New York State line.

A little under an hour later he had sighted the field where the Silver Flash had been found, and was coasting down toward the group of figures on the north side. As a matter of fact, though, even in the middle of summer that spot of ground could not exactly be termed a field.

It was more a part of a timber slope, that had been cleared

for reasons known only to the owner of the property. Several tree stumps stuck up above the drift snow. And in places there were the snow-covered humps of boulders that, like icebergs, concealed seven tenths of their size. But field or no field, the Silver Flash was there. And as Curly caught sight of the glistening craft a choking lump rose up in his throat.

Cursing, by way of giving relief to his inner feelings, he banked around to the long side of the slope and set the twin-engined craft down in a perfect exhibition of piloting. By the time he had the cabin door open and was leaping out, several of the group had detached themselves from the others and were running over.

An infantry colonel was leading them. But Curly gave him only a flash glance and went plowing through the snow over to Dusty's plane. He did not even know that Biff was at his heels until the big pilot bumped into him as he skidded to a stop beside the cockpit.

"Gee, Curly, what are we gonna do? We got to do something!"

Curly didn't bother to answer. He had climbed up on the fuselage step and was staring narrow eyed at the interior of the cockpit. Last night Dusty had been sitting there on that seat—had his hands on that spade-grip stick—his feet on those rudder pedals. And now, he was gone. Gone—leaving behind only stains of his blood where he had smashed his head against the glass dial of the alcohol compass.

SLOWLY BROOKS stepped down, turned and gazed at dragging marks in the snow that led down the slope for some thirty yards to a set of ski-wheel landing gear tracks. With his eye he followed them across the snow to a point where they stopped—the point of take-off of the mysterious plane. From there he raised his eyes toward the slaty, snow-cloud-laden heavens and heaved a long, bitter sigh.

"Say, kid, I've been thinking."

The rumble of Biff Bolton's voice at his ear shook Curly out of his trance.

"Yeah? Thinking about what? We've all been thinking—and nothing else!"

Bill put out a protesting hand.

"Now, that's no way, Curly!" he chided. "Get hold of yourself, lad. Listen about what Jack Horner was saying—about that Rocky Mountain, idea. There may be something to it at that, you know."

He seemed to stop for lack of words. Curly frowned at him.

"Maybe you're right," he said. "I haven't forgotten, myself, what Jack said. But, dammit, who nabbed Dusty?"

He gave it up with a savage grunt of self-disgust. Then suddenly he whirled and leaped up on the fuselage step again. He was back in the snow in almost a continuance of the same movement.

"Those fake cylinders of Metal-Meltic!" he yelped at Biff, grabbing his arm. "They're down there on the cockpit floor—down there with the flare chute. The bum, whoever he is, passed them up."

"Then that settles it!" The voice of Jack Horner roared out behind Curly and Biff. They turned as the Intelligence man came running up, face flushed with excitement.

"Yes, that's the answer!" he went on before either Biff or Curly could say anything. "Don't you see? He found out that they were fake—realized that the whole thing was a trap. So, instead of killing Dusty, he did the obvious thing!"

"Obvious what?" the other two cut in in the same breath.

"Kidnaped Dusty!" young Horner bellowed. "Took him along as hostage. Get it—we send back our prisoner if you send us the real formula! Not as crude as that, of course. But something along that line. Or, maybe they think Dusty knows more about the thing than he does. One thing's certain, though—they don't know that we haven't the complete formula either! That'll give us some time, at least!"

"Time?" snapped Curly. "We don't need time! What we need is an inkling of where they've taken Dusty, so that we can go there and get him. Listen, this Rocky Mountain angle—just what do you think about that, Jack? Have you any real proof? I mean, anything to work on?"

The Intelligence man didn't answer directly. He half turned and looked across the slope to where the infantry colonel and a few others were engaged in conversation with Major Drake. When he turned back, there was an annoyed expression on his lean face.

"I have only the report of our own agents," he snapped out bluntly. "And I put a lot of stock in their reports. Regardless of what Major Drake said, there is something screwy going on in the southwestern Montana area.

"Hell, when the war broke out, we didn't know that the Blacks had holed up in the Hudson Bay area, did we? No, but they had just the same. Well, what the hell would stop them from pulling the same stunt on a smaller plan in some out-of-the-way place in the Rockies? Because of this damn snow, both sides are more or less marking time."

"But what good would it do to park troops there?" Biff butted in. "The Rockies ain't those Canadian plateaus, Jack."

The Intelligence man snorted wrathfully.

"For God's sake!" he yelled, "have I got to tell you airmen that ground troops aren't everything in this war? How—"

"An air base!" Curly roared. "A secret air base for gas and germ bombing!"

"Now you're showing what sense you've got!" Horner snapped. "Sure, a secret air base. Or maybe it's something like they had down there at Chihuahua, Mexico. There's no telling just what it might be. I'm simply saying that—"

"That," Curly broke in again, "our best bet in finding Dusty is that southwest Montana area of the Rockies. And, by God, that's where I'm going. I'm going to smoke out the works from one end to the other—until I find Dusty!"

"Wait a minute, Curly," spoke up Jack Horner. "That's a lot of territory out there. One plane and one pilot wouldn't be able to do much."

"Hell, I'm going along, too!" boomed Biff.

"Two planes wouldn't do much!" the Intelligence man went on evenly. "As I was about to say, I suggest that we organize a general search. Ten or fifteen air units, contacting ground parties."

Curly stopped him with a vigorous shake of his head.

"It would take too long to get organized," he said. "I've got a better plan, a plan that may work just as I hope it will. I'm going to make the search in this ship—Dusty's Flash!"

He paused to let the underlying meaning sink in. Young Horner simply grimaced, and Biff Bolton blinked.

"What do you expect that to get you?" the Intelligence man asked. "Just because you're flying his ship isn't going to help you find out where he is any quicker!"

"No?" Brooks bit off. "You're missing the point! If he is somewhere down in that region, and he sees the Flash, he'll know we've got an idea where he is, and are trying to get to him. Maybe he'll be able to signal me in some way.

"Secondly, if the ones who grabbed him are down there, too, they'll figure it the same way—figure that we're wise to their presence in that region. That will put the next move up to them. They'll either come out in the open and make a break for it, or else they'll try to hole up even tighter.

"Either way, it will be to our benefit. We'll be able to get a darn good line on them, one way or the other. Hell, using Dusty's plane is the one perfect thing about the whole plan. You know, get the other guy worried and he's bound to make a wrong step. Your way, Jack, might take us weeks, and get us nowhere. Yup! I'm going to take the Flash and go to work."

"I still think that the two of us could do it better," Biff stuck in doggedly.

But Curly shook his head.

"Your turn will come later, kid," he said. "At the start it's a one-man job. You fly Jack and the major back to the field. There's just a chance, you know, that Dusty will get through to us direct at the field. That is, if he's still—dammit, I know he is! He's got to be alive.

"Watch it! Here comes the major. I haven't got time to argue with him. Don't think he'd like the idea any better than you two do. But shut up! For once, I'm going to play something my way!"

He had hardly finished when the C.O. reached them.

"Can't say that coming up here helped any, Brooks!" he snapped at Curly. "We learned everything there was to learn, over the radio. But maybe you've got another bright idea?"

Curly looked crestfallen.

"Nothing much, sir," he said with a shrug. "But if it's okay with you, I'll fly his ship back. I kind of think that he'd like to have me do that. Like they said, it's in good shape."

The C.O. gave him a keen look, also included Jack Horner and Biff Bolton.

"Is that what you've been wrangling about?" he shot out. "Heard you from way over there!"

"No, sir," Curly answered truthfully, at the same time climbing up on the fuselage step. "We were arguing about the whole thing in general—wondering if he might possibly get in touch with us direct, at the field."

"Then you feel sure he's still alive?"

"I feel surer than ever that he's still alive, sir," Curly came right back. "Look, sir, they must have got wise to the whole thing. So they took Dusty, instead of this!"

As he spoke the last, Brooks reached down into the cockpit

with both hands, heaved up the empty tanks and the flare parachute, and dumped them down into the snow.

"Okay, stand clear!" he called out right afterward. "I'm going to start her up!"

Out of the corner of his eye he saw an expression of puzzled suspicion spread over Major Drake's face. Instantly he slid down into the cockpit, kept his head bent and thumped down on the electric starter.

"Come on, Silver Flash!" he whispered fiercely. "Let's get going and away—before the major changes his mind!"

Twice, Curly desperately booted the electric starter, and twice the engine didn't give forth a single murmur. The third time it caught, however, and roared into life. But it was at that exact moment that Curly sensed someone climbing up on the fuselage step. He raised his head and stared into Major Drake's narrowed eyes, and his heart went sliding down into his boots.

He gulped, tried to look innocent.

"Yes sir?" weakly.

"There never was a pilot that I couldn't read like a book, Brooks!" came the startling words. "But I'm not fool enough to try to stop any crazy plan that's in your mind, at the moment. Only—only, for God's sake watch your step, son. Losing one of you is too much as it is! Luck!"

With that, the C.O. jumped down from the step and walked quickly off to the side.

CHAPTER 6
THE SCARLET ACE

THREE MINUTES later, Curly eased open the throttle of the Flash, taxied a few feet to shake the clinging snow from the ski-wheel landing gear, and then with a quick wave to those watching he rammed the throttle wide open. Like something human, and overjoyed to be in motion again, the Silver Flash virtually leaped forward across the glistening whiteness.

The twenty-eight hundred horses cowled into the nose thundered out a mighty song of power, and after a run of but a few short yards the plane responded instantly to Curly's touch and went streaking off the slope and up toward the lead-gray clouds.

Holding the ship on its maximum climbing angle, Curly took time out to slam the cockpit cowl shut and seal it with the locking lugs. Then he carefully checked the instruments for temporary faults. But finding them in perfect working order, he slumped back comfortably in the seat and kept one eye on the air above, and the other on the altimeter dial and drift indicator.

At thirty-two thousand feet, exactly, he found what he wanted—a stiff thirty-mile-an-hour wind on his tail from the last. There he leveled off, swung in robot control and let the mechanical pilot do the work for him.

"Now, let's see," he mused aloud, glancing at his wrist watch. "With a stop at St. Paul for fuel—just in case—I should hit the mountains between two and three. That'll give me a couple of hours light. Damn—wish I'd started this thing sooner!"

Thoughts of the last irked him. And, as though he could do better himself, he swung off robot control and took charge. Hunching forward over the stick he silently cursed the plane on to greater speed.

For over an hour he flew due west between two great cloud layers that stretched to the four horizons. Through the top layer filtered a bit of the sun's light, with the result that he seemed to be thundering along an endless corridor of shimmering gold.

The weird beauty of it had no effect upon him, however. Other and far more important things occupied the attention of his mind. Each passing minute was but another minute of worry about the fate of his closest pal. Like the unrolling of a motion-picture reel, every incident of their years together flashed vividly across his brain. So vivid, that each incident seemed to have happened only yesterday. And, eventually, he reached the final picture—a picture of the very plane in which he now sat, hurtling earthward through night skies tinged with flaming blue!

Hardly realizing it, he smashed his free fist against the side of the cockpit, groaned aloud. And it was at that moment that the red signal light on the radio panel blinked furiously.

One glance, and he knew that some station was signaling on the S.O.S. Emergency wave-length reading. Realization and action were one for him. He whipped out his hand, snapped up the switch, and spun the dial.

The ear-phones crackled out sound instantly.

"Calling all planes North Central Areas! Calling all planes in North Central Areas! Corbin of Unit Twenty. Strange all-red enemy monoplane pursuit above me—flying due west toward Dakota border. Unable to reach it. Suggest that you try and—wait, wait—it's coming down—"

The voice trailed off into throbbing silence that lasted perhaps a full minute. Then the ear-phones gave off a shrill, piercing scream. It was like the scream of a half crazed man who has met with some horrible catastrophe. Just one ten-second scream, and then clicking sound in the ear-phones, signifying that the set at the other end had either been snapped off, or had gone dead by accident.

For a couple of moments Curly sat perfectly stiff, staring at the radio panel, and half expecting to hear more sounds from the ear-phones. Presently he did hear more sounds. But they were simply the broadcasts of a dozen different stations trying to check-back on the broadcaster who had said he was Corbin of Unit Twenty.

A quick glance at the station direction finder told Curly that he was a good eight hundred to a thousand miles from the point of the original broadcast. Too far away, anyway, for him to be of any help—if help was now needed.

Nevertheless, he changed his course slightly and went thundering toward that spot. And as he tore through the air, part of the wild message repeated itself over and over again inside his head—all red monoplane pursuit—all red monoplane pursuit flying due west toward Dakota border!

"Which one?" he shouted aloud to himself. "North Dakota,

or South Dakota?" Then, still aloud, "Nuts! What difference does it make? It looks like Jack was right! Looks like I'm right, too."

Oblivious to the cackling of a dozen different radio operators in the earphones, he went thundering tail-up down the cloud lanes. Minutes dragged by, became an hour, then an hour and a half. The radio cackling had long since died away, but he was not even conscious that it was gone. As a matter of fact, he was not conscious of anything save his calculated position every other three or four minutes.

Finally, he stuck the nose down and went careening through the lower cloud layers into clear air. With a grunt of grim satisfaction he noted from the terrain below that he had smacked his objective right on the nose.

He was right over the intersection of Montana and North and South Dakota. In other words, in the same section of sky whence had come the wild call for help—assuming, of course, that the Flash's station direction finder had functioned properly.

BUT IF he expected to see anything startling—anything such as an all-red Black Invader pursuit monoplane floating around in lazy circles—he was doomed to instant disappointment. There wasn't the single sign of a plane in the air below the clouds. And five minutes later, when he had climbed up through four layers to sunlight-filled clear air, he found the same thing to be true up above.

Impulsively he shot out his free hand to spin the wave-length dial and contact a local station for information. But before his fingers touched the knob, he changed his mind and let his hand drop back into his lap.

"No sense to that," he grunted aloud. "Probably don't know any more than I do. Besides, it's the red crate you want. Get going!"

A glance at the fuel gauge showed that although he had passed up a landing at St. Paul, he still had enough in the tanks for five to six more hours of flying. To go back to St. Paul, or to any other field for that matter, would be more or less of a waste of precious daylight.

His mind made up, he swung the Flash around and went thundering west over the Montana line. In his original excitement he had thought only of reaching the Rockies. But now, as he neared the section of which Jack Horner had spoken, he realized the seemingly utter futility of the task he had set for himself.

He smashed his fist down on one knee.

"Unless they see the Flash, and tip their hand!" he breathed fiercely, "I'm sunk! No, like hell I am! I'll find Dusty no matter where he is!"

Repeating the last over and over again, to bolster up his failing spirits, he urged the plane on to greater speed, and kept his eyes glued on the distant horizon. For a full hour he kept well above the clouds. And then, finally, when a careful check of his instruments placed him within gliding distance of the northern end of the Big Belt mountain range, he eased back the throttle and went coasting down through the clouds.

The instant he came out he checked his position, found that

once again he had hit it right on the nose, and then concentrated on a minute study of the terrain below.

The first look brought a bitter laugh to his lips. A minute study? Hell, he could spend a week in a minute study of only one square mile! And there were a good five hundred miles to be searched.

Save for three or four cities, stuck here and there among the towering snow-covered peaks, the terrain in general was an over-awing expanse of rugged, impenetrable wilderness reaching to the four horizons. A gigantic panorama of Nature untouched and unconquered by man since the very beginning of time.

As he gazed down hopelessly at the scene the words of Jack Horner filtered through his brain—"You could hide half a hundred army corps in that area, and nobody would be the wiser!"

Hell, yes! And then some. And with the additional protection of the great blanket of snow, the region was practically a world all by itself—a world that could only be entered by air, and left by the same way.

"But there could be a hundred hidden dromes down there!"

The words burst unconsciously from his lips, as he banked south, opened the throttle and went roaming over the interwoven network of jagged, glistening peaks.

"Yeah!" he echoed his own words. "And you're just making a sap of yourself, Brooks! Jack was right—one plane can't do this job. It needs a hundred, two hundred—and a lot more!"

With a bitter groan he reached out for the wave-length knob

to call his home field and tell young Horner to start organizing a concentrated air and ground search at once. But, as though it had almost been planned by unseen powers, his fingers had hardly touched the knob when the red signal light blinked.

As his eyes flew to the incoming station recorder, he jerked up straight in the seat. Some station was signaling for contact on the wave-length of the Silver Flash's set—the personal wave-length of Dusty Ayres.

For a second he could not force his fingers to snap on the contact switch and twist the dial. He gulped out a curse, broke the weird spell that gripped him, made contact and grabbed up the transmitter tube.

"Contact made!" he shouted. "Go ahead!"

There was a moment of silence, and then a voice crackled in the ear-phones—a voice that made Curly's heart do wild loops in his chest. It was the voice of Dusty Ayres!

"Ayres calling! Who is flying my ship?"

Curly nearly cut his lips as he jammed the transmitter tube against them in his wild excitement.

"Dusty! Dusty! This is Curly—Curly Brooks! Where are you, kid? I've been looking for you! Are you all right? Where are you, Dusty?"

"I'm okay!" came back the answer. "Every thing's fine! So, it's you, eh? Good boy! Listen, does anyone else know where you are?"

"Huh?" echoed Brooks. "What do you mean?"

"I mean, do any of the others know your present position?

Are you by yourself? Or are there other ships around—American ships?"

"No, I'm alone," Curly told him. "And nobody knows my exact present position—not unless they are listening in on us now. And only Jack and Biff know my general location. But where are you, Dusty? Your signals are coming from the ground. For God's sake, where are you?"

"Don't talk so much!" the ear-phones snapped back. "Listen, I've got to hurry. Now do just as I tell you. Keep on this wavelength, and fly as I order. Right?"

"Right! Where do I fly? Which way?"

"Keep going as you are now," said the ear-phones. "But throttle and come closer to earth. I can only just see you in the glasses. Come down a bit."

Curly glanced ahead, saw the peaks of the Gallatin Range.

"Straight ahead toward the—"

"Shut up!" the ear-phones barked savagely. "Don't let your position go out over the air. Come down lower!"

OBEDIENTLY, CURLY eased back the throttle and sent the Flash sliding down toward the treacherous terrain below him. Lower and lower he went, expecting to hear Dusty's voice again in the next second. Finally, when he was but a few hundred feet above a group of peaks that formed the rim of a half-mile-wide crater formation, he was about to speak himself, when Dusty's voice came to him again.

"Bank right and fly toward the other side of what you see below you!"

"Right it is!" he called, and moved the controls.

The maneuver resulted in a due west course across the top of the crater. But as he glanced ahead, he saw that the peaks on the west side towered a good three to four thousand feet above the others.

To fly between them—if that was what he had to do—would be one tricky job. Air current would toss him about like a cork in a heavy gale. True, the terrific speed of the Flash would help plenty. But even then, it would call for everything he had.

The thought caused him to unconsciously nose up the ship toward the top of the peaks. But instantly Dusty's voice barked at him.

"Don't climb, you dope! Keep on coming down!"

Curly corrected his error as the voice continued.

"Now, look—straight ahead. See that tallest peak?"

"Right!"

"See the third to the right of it?"

Curly looked to the left, saw the peak mentioned.

"Okay!" he grunted.

"Good!" grunted the voice in the earphones. "Now between it and the next there is a shelf about halfway down. Land at the wide end, toward those trees. Can you do it?"

It took Curly a couple of minutes to find the shelf-like platform of rock halfway down the mountain side. But for Dusty's instructions, he would never have spotted it in a thousand years.

It was about three thousand feet below the summer snow line. And now, with its timbered fringes covered with snow, it

A SLEDGE HAMMER SMASHED AGAINST CURLY'S CHEST.

appeared as a part of the slope, rather than being a shelf that jutted out between the mountains.

But as he peered at it hard, he knew that he could sit the Flash down on it without a great deal of trouble. The surrounding mountains served as a sort of channel for the wind, forcing it along parallel with the shelf.

"Can do easy!" he said into the transmitter tube.

"Then go ahead!" came the reply. "Land, cut your engine. Then get out and wait. No—move over close to those trees. Okay! I'll be waiting."

Heart beating wildly at the thought of an immediate reunion with his pal, Curly slapped the Flash around and down toward the mountain shelf.

A bit of a cross-wind caught him and drove him off his course for a moment. But easing open the throttle a bit and applying rudder instantly, counteracted the cross-wind effect. And like the bullet from a gun he went streaking straight down toward the shelf.

As he neared it, flattened out a bit for the landing, he noticed that the snow on the shelf had been packed down. Instead of it being in drifting heaps, it had been smoothed out level and packed. Realization jerked his eyes open wide, and he searched the plateau formation for—he didn't know just what.

In the back of his brain he dully realized that considerable time had been spent on packing the snow—and that without question it was used as some sort of an airdrome. Yet, in the time allowed, he saw not the slightest sign of any planes.

On the south side the mountain towered up toward the

clouds—a massive slab of snow covered rock, dotted here and there by a few trees. Two hundred feet out from the mountain-side the shelf tilted off at a four-degree angle until it met the flanking mountain. In a way, the shelf was more of a long narrow tray of rock between the flanking mountain sides.

At least, that was the impression he got as he sent the Flash streaking in. The job of landing right side up prohibited any second impressions. Hands and feet working in perfect coordination, he slid the plane down the last hundred feet, flattened out and settled. With a swishing, crunching sound the ski-wheels hit the packed snow. The Flash bounced twice, and would have gone swerving crazily off on right wing—toward the edge of the shelf—had not Curly jerked it in time. Slamming on opposite rudder, and "gunning" the engine, he pulled the craft back on its course and went sliding and bouncing across the snow to a full stop.

The instant movement ceased, he snapped off the engine, unlocked the self sealing lugs, pushed back the cockpit cowl and leaped out. A blast of icy air swirled around him, cut through the heavy flying togs he wore. It was like jumping from an overheated room into a tub full of cracked ice.

But he noticed the difference in temperature just long enough to curse. Then he started running toward the snow-laden trees at the far end.

At every step he expected to see the familiar figure of Dusty come dashing out to meet him. But no familiar figure appeared. And finally, when he reached the edge of the trees and skidded to a halt, he was still all alone on the wintery shelf. In fact, for all the companionship he had at that moment, he might just as well be a hundred miles from the government meteorological station at the North Pole.

Frowning, he cast his eyes about for a moment, then cupped his hands to his mouth.

"Hey! Hey, Dusty! Where—"

He sensed, rather than saw the movement behind him. He spun around, a grin on his face.

"Gosh! You had me worried for a—"

The grin on his face froze. Under the trees, not twenty yards from him stood three figures—three figures in the uniform of Black Invaders. And in the clenched right hand of each figure was a gun.

For a split second Curly blinked stupidly, Then the bellow of an enraged bull gushed from his throat.

"Damn you!"

His right hand streaked down for his holstered gun, and in the same movement he flung his body to one side. But he never touched his gun. There was a spurt of flame, and the sharp crack of sound. A sledgehammer smashed against Curly's chest. His body was knocked clear of the snow, and he had the weird, crazy, split-second impression that he was shooting out into space—shooting out like the projectile of a naval gun!

CHAPTER 7
ZYTOFF

"**I** WOULDN'T try to move, Captain Ayres! In the first place, you see, it's quite impossible. Just sit still, and you'll be far more comfortable!"

From out of a whirlpool of darkness came the words, beating against Dusty's throbbing brain like so many white hot trip-hammers. Gradually light pierced the darkness, and in a befuddled, abstract sort of way, he realized that he was staring at the instrument board of an airplane. An instrument board covered with countless gadgets just barely visible in the faint glow of a small cowl lamp.

He closed his eyes tight, gritted his teeth against a horrible pain on the top of his head, then opened his eyes again. The instrument board was still in front of him, and just above it, the forward end of reinforced glass cowling that sloped back over his head.

"The instruments interest you, captain? Or haven't you recovered yet from that rather nasty crack on the head?"

A voice to his left—cool, calm, dripping with self-assurance, yet not blatantly so. He started to turn his head, but stopped as the top of it seemed to rip off. He tried again, steeled himself against the pain, and succeeded.

A man swathed in fur-lined flying clothes sat beside him. He was smiling pleasantly, and there was what might be taken for an amused twinkle in his deep-sunk, jet-black eyes.

As a matter of fact, the stranger's entire expression was one of contented amusement. Pain forgotten for the moment, Dusty swept him with his eyes from helmeted head to heavy-soled boots resting on rudder pedals. During that moment he realized that he was in the double cockpit of a plane, and that the plane was tearing along through night-darkened skies.

"Say! What the hell? Where am I?"

Dusty's words echoing back to him were the only indication that he had spoken them. His brain, as far as grasping what the situation in which he found himself was all about, was a total blank.

He saw the stranger lean forward and glance at the instruments a moment, then turn flashing teeth upon him.

"Just rest awhile, captain," the man said. "Just rest, and try to collect yourself. You're still very dizzy!"

A queer quirk of the brain caused Dusty to take the last as a dirty crack. He tried to sit up straight. But it was then that he got his third surprise in a row. Both wrists were lashed securely to the metal bars of the seat. His ankles, also, were lashed and tied back so that they were out of the way of the nearest rudder pedal. The shock cleared his head a bit, and he cursed aloud.

"Who the hell are you!" he grated. "And what's this all about? The last thing I remember, I was—"

Like the flood waters of a bursting dam, memory came racing back to him. The Silver Flash! He was flying toward P Fourteen! Some one ordered him to fly north. He'd tried to get out from under. There'd been a swirling blue cyclone in the night sky. A sizzling, terrific heat! He hadn't been able to get clear of it! He'd gone spinning down, and he'd—yeah, he must have crashed.

He cut short on his thoughts, scowled into the grinning face at his side.

"So you're the little boy scout who is responsible, eh?" he gulped.

Broad shoulders shrugged, and more white teeth flashed as the stranger widened his grin.

"Not entirely, captain," the man said. "I'd say that your lucky star is mostly responsible. Just why you are still alive is something that I'll never be able to answer correctly. An overwhelming amount of luck, and perfect flying, I guess. My compliments on the latter, by the way. You are even better than they told me you were."

"They?" echoed Dusty in a flat voice.

"Those who have met you, and lived," came the reply. "I suppose that makes me one of them now. But I must say that tonight's little venture wasn't exactly difficult. Shall we call it, say—child's play?"

As the man talked Dusty studied his face. Tried to fathom the brain working behind the twinkling eyes. That the man was a Black, or at least connected with the Invaders, was a self-evident truth.

Yet his mannerisms, his tone of speech, the very atmosphere he created, set him as far apart from a Black as chalk is from cheese. No bragging, no blustering and snarling, or anything approaching it. The man spoke just as anyone might speak during a casual conversation with a friend.

81

In spite of the weirdness of the situation, Dusty grinned and shrugged his bewilderment.

"I'll hand it to you for coolness, buzzard," he said. "And no argument about it. Just for the hell of it, though, would you mind answering my question? What in hell is this all about? Up to now, I'm supposed to have crashed. Don't tell me that this is what we meet in the life after!"

The other threw back his head and laughed loudly.

"And I hand it to you for being cool, captain," he chuckled. "I'm almost sorry that I tied you up. From reports of your former deeds, I thought it best to apply the safety first theory. But seriously, you didn't exactly crash. As I said, by some miracle— and a lot of fine flying—you escaped my attempt to kill you. Incidentally, you may recall my telling you over the radio that I was reluctant to kill you?"

"Yeah. Thanks."

"No thanks needed, my friend. I really did not want to kill you. But—well, it seemed necessary. I later discovered my mistake. It would seem that both of us were trying to pull off a little *coup de grace* tonight. And to a measure, we were both very neatly fooled.

"You did not expect what happened, and I did not expect to find that you did not carry that which I wanted. But, as I was saying, or about to say, you dropped a landing flare and succeeded in making a rather decent landing. And—"

"I dropped a landing flare? I don't remember that!"

"But you did—a small one. I landed close to you and when I reached your plane I found you quite unconscious. In some way you'd been thrown forward. You cracked your head on the compass. Very convenient for me, if you'll pardon the expression?"

"Skip it," Dusty grunted. "And then? How come I'm still able to take nourishment? There are plenty of your breed who would have pulled a trigger. In other words, why didn't you? Why the kidnap act? It is a kidnap act, isn't it? Sort of taking home the bacon to old man Fire-Eyes, eh? Betcha get a swell medal for this."

THE BLACK didn't answer directly. Ignoring Dusty he concentrated on checking the plane's position, and compass course. But when he looked at Dusty again there was a slight glint of disappointment in place of the twinkle in his eye.

"Conceit does not become you, captain," he said quietly. "In fact, it's entirely out of place in your make-up. A medal? No! You are far more valuable to me than any medal. Yes, far more valuable. Frankly, there was a reason for your little trick to-night—a trick that came very close to working, by the way. I intend to find out that reason. Find out several things."

Dusty looked dumb.

"Trick?" he echoed. "What trick?"

The smile came back to the other's face. It was almost a paternal type of smile.

"Those empty gas cylinders, and the flare chute," the Black said. "You were out for a bit of bomb-dropping practice, perhaps?"

The Yank grinned.

"How'd you guess? Got it the first time. By the way, you didn't bring them along did you?"

Dusty twisted around as much as he could, looked back and

83

stiffened. The rear wall of the semi-cabin cockpit was about a foot in back of him. It was blank save for near the top where there was a set of valve handles, some lengths of pipe running from them up through the top of the cabin, and a couple of pressure dials. At least, he took the dialed instruments to be pressure recorders.

"No," he heard the Black answer his question. "I did not bring them along. What use would they be to me? Yet I can't complain, I guess. I've brought you along instead. And I feel that you can tell me considerably more than those gas tanks could tell me—even though they had been full of your precious Metal-Meltic!"

Dusty snapped back front, fixed his eyes on the man.

"You know everything, don't you?" he grunted.

"No, not everything. For instance, the whereabouts of the real formula. Perhaps you can tell me where Major Crandall put it before he died so suddenly?"

Though the man's knowledge of the drama of Metal-Meltic made Dusty's heart thump wildly against his ribs, he kept his face expressionless. At the same time, however, he became instantly on the alert.

"So you don't know that, eh?" he said in a meaning tone. "Well, that's certainly one on us, I must say! Huh! And all the time we've been thinking that you birds had tapped that second batch and that Morgan had told you about the new formula. Hell, you might as well put me down on the ground. Then we all can start the act over again."

Dusty spoke the crazy thoughts just as they came to him.

But as he looked into the other's face he realized that they were bearing fruit. For one thing, a lot of the man's self assurance went out of his being.

His eyes narrowed in half suspicion and half puzzlement and they bored searchingly into Dusty's. In other words, the Black was swinging at three wild curves, and not realizing that they were bad ones.

"So Morgan knew about the new formula?" he put the question softly, as though to himself. "Then why didn't he say—"

"Because I didn't give him the chance," Dusty cut in. "So now we're right back where we started—or are we?"

The Black pressed his lips together in a gesture of heavy thought, grunted through his nose.

"Perhaps," he said. "We shall see, presently."

Dusty grinned. He couldn't possibly feel any worse, so he was beginning to feel better. At least mentally, for the moment.

"Here's hoping, in case not," Dusty grinned. "But in the meantime, do you happen to have a flask? A good shot would help this dome of mine a lot."

He spoke just for the sake of saying something, but to his amazement the Black reached into a cabin wall pocket and drew forth a flask. Snapping off the cap he turned and held it to Dusty's lips.

It was fine old brandy, and as it slipped down his throat Dusty began to feel one hundred per cent better. A nod of his head signaled the Black to take the flask away. Dusty coughed on the last couple of drops, got his breath back and billowed his cheeks.

"Thanks!" he breathed. "That did help!"

Then twisting toward the Black:

"Surprise number umpty-seven!" he exclaimed with a puzzled frown. "I would have bet the roll against your doing what you did just now. Say, who are you anyway? Not the little fairy who rescued the princess from the old duffer with the tobacco-stained beard?"

A twisted smile came to the other's lips.

"You find me different from the Hawk, or Ekar, eh?" he murmured.

Dusty nodded vigorously.

"Very much so! In fact, you strike me as a chap who has made a hell of a dumb mistake!"

"I've what?"

"Made a hell of a dumb mistake and don't know it!" Dusty repeated. "You enlisted on the wrong side. You should be an American!"

"So? Perhaps you are forgetting, captain, that I tried very hard to kill you tonight."

Dusty shrugged.

"Call it a part of your contract," he grunted. "Anyway I'm skipping it, for the present. Now for the big surprise—who are you? As we say down Dixie way—yuh have the advantage of me, suh!"

"I doubt that my name would mean anything to you, Captain Ayres," was the quiet reply. "As you mimic, I have the advantage of you, in several ways. But all that is a result of training and experience. A name means very little to me. As a matter of fact,

I've used several different names during my life. Some years ago, when I took a post-graduate course at Harvard, I was known as Davenport—R. J. Davenport."

"Ah!" nodded Dusty. "I knew there was something familiar about your accent. Harvard, eh? Well, I refuse to hold that against you. But to bring everything up to date—what's the name now? I might want to introduce you to some of my friends, you know."

THE BLACK chuckled, squinted at his instruments again. Dusty took a squint, too. He noted that the plane was flying a few degrees north of true west, and at a high altitude. Then the Black gave him his attention again.

"Your last remark is doubtful," he said. "However, I shall probably meet Lieutenant Brooks and Lieutenant Horner eventually."

The last surprised Dusty, and he showed it. Impulsively he leaned toward the Black, his face strained.

"My ship!" he snapped. "It was the only one that went down?"

"Then I was correct, eh? There were other planes near you! Yes, captain, your ship was the only one that went down."

Dusty slumped back against the seat, stared narrow-eyed at the instrument board and tried to think. The result was not very exhilarating. Underneath all the chit-chat he had been carrying on with this strange Black was a deeper meaning. Something was in the wind.

He couldn't put his finger on it, right at the moment. But he knew that all this palaver was but a preliminary act for something really important. The Black expected him to talk; spill what he knew, or what the Black thought he knew. Hell no, the man wasn't that dumb! Okay—then, so what? Why was he—

The Black broke in on his jumble of thoughts.

"And now that we've passed the time very pleasantly, captain," he said. "I must ask you to hold still while I blindfold your eyes. Yes, we will be landing soon."

The man had released his hold on the stick and was folding a handkerchief kitty-corner. In the few seconds allowed, Dusty snapped his eyes toward the instrument board. Though the instruments were graduated in Black Invader units of measure, he had seen enough similar ones before to be able to read them more or less accurately. He noted that the plane was flying a course considerably south of the U.S.-Canadian line, and that they were over the Rocky Mountain areas.

The Black must have guessed the reason for the puzzled look that came over Dusty's face, for he shrugged indifferently.

"Don't worry, captain," he said. "I know exactly where we are."

Dusty forced a grin to his lips, fired what he believed to be a jolting shot.

"And so do our ground detectors downstairs!"

The Black blinked for a second, then broke into a hearty laugh.

"Yes, yes, captain, you're absolutely correct. But I don't believe that those manning the ground detectors will get overly curious."

"No?"

"No. I'm not exactly that stupid. You see, I had this craft fitted with an engine of American design! In daylight my plans depend upon speed. At night they depend upon your country-men believing that an American plane is flying over them. And now, hold still please."

With deft fingers the man covered Dusty's eyes with the folded handkerchief and tied it securely in back.

"Sorry that you cannot watch me land, captain," came the words to Dusty's ears. "But you'll just have to put your trust in my flying ability."

The Yank grunted.

"I might," he said, "if I knew who you were."

He heard the Black chuckle softly, Then—

"Still curious, eh?"

"Yeah! Still curious. But if you think I might use it against you, why—"

"Oh, it really doesn't matter one way or the other," the Black broke in on him. "My name's Zytoff."

CHAPTER 8
SHOW-DOWN

ZYTOFF! LIKE a streak of blue lightning, Dusty's memory raced back over the weeks to that day when he and Agent 10 and Curly Brooks had helped wipe out the Black Troposphere Flying Submarine base at Bersimis on the St. Lawrence.

It had been on that day, the very day that Ekar, the Avenger, had died, that he had first heard of the name, Zytoff. Jack Horner had told him—told him of a mysterious Black Invader leader who had risen to a position of highest favor with Fire-Eyes. That man was known as Zytoff.

It was he who was to have complete command of the Tropo-Submarine armada. At the time he was supposed to be still in Europe—waiting there for final word from Fire-Eyes to begin his crushing attack against the U.S. Naval and coast defense forces.

The destruction of the Bersimis base had obviously postponed any such attack. Undoubtedly it was because the U.S. had captured the last remaining Troposphere F-S, and had immediately begun construction of a similar type of war craft for its own use. Yes, with the element of mystery and surprise gone, the Blacks had postponed their action.

But! Zytoff had come to the United States. Zytoff, the mysterious, was here in the country! Perhaps he had been here for some time. But even more important, perhaps, right now he was coasting a plane for a landing on American ground and one Yank pilot was coasting down with him!

"You have heard of me, captain?"

The question snapped Dusty away from his depressing reminiscences. "Nope, can't say that I have," he lied.

"I didn't think so," was the quiet comment. "But I believe that now that you have, you and all of your countrymen will be a long time forgetting it!"

With that somewhat ominous statement the Black stopped talking. Dusty didn't say anything more either, just sat perfectly still and pictured in his mind the plane rushing down through night skies toward the ground.

Once he heard Zytoff snap something in his native lingo. It could have been some annoyed remark made out loud, or it could have been the man contacting somebody over the radio. A second later, when Dusty thought he heard the click of the switch, he felt positive that Zytoff had used the radio.

ZYTOFF

Presently, he felt the plane come out of its dive; knew that it had leveled off and that they were banking to the right. Then he heard the hiss of a compressed air chute flare being released. He felt the plane bank a bit to the right, straighten out, and settle lightly with hardly a, jar. Instinctively, he nodded his head in appreciation of what he knew was a damn good landing—no matter where the landing had been made.

"Thank you, captain," came Zytoff's pleasant voice to his ears. "And now, I must give you a warning. I am going to release your hands and feet, but not the blindfold. Make no attempt to remove it, and do just as you are instructed. You understand?"

"You're the doctor," Dusty grunted. Then added, "For the moment."

"For a considerably longer time than that!" was the somewhat sharp comment. "Very well, hold still."

The sudden release of pressure about Dusty's wrists and ankles told him that they had been freed of their bonds. A second later strong fingers gripped his arm, pulled him up on his feet.

A blast of icy wind smacked against his face, sent violent shivers all the way down to his toes. He heard several voices speaking in Black Invader. More hands gripped him and he was lifted into the air. When his feet touched something solid again, he knew that it was hard-pack snow.

Both arms held tightly, he was led forward. Something slapped against his face, stung his cheek and dropped coldness down under the collar of his flying suit. It might have been a snow-laden branch. He didn't stop to figure it out.

Though his eyes were blindfolded, he knew that he had been ushered into some sort of a lighted room. The cold wind wasn't tugging at him now. He felt quite comfortable. Those holding him, however, did not stop. They continued to lead him forward; now right, now left, and now down a short flight of stairs.

From the sound he knew that they were wooden stairs. The floor over which they had led him, had been wooden, too. Those deductions placed him in some sort of a house. A house with several rooms. He was sure of that, because at intervals had heard doors open on either side; heard voices located a short distance away.

Eventually, his escort pulled him to a stop and pushed him down into a chair. Then the handkerchief was whisked away from his eyes. The sudden change made him blink, and for a moment his surroundings were all a mixed-up jumble of golden shades.

Presently, though, his eyes became adjusted to the light from a ceiling lamp, and he found himself seated in a fairly large room—sitting at a table covered with food. There were no windows in the room, that is, no windows with glass. At the top of the far wall there was an opening. No light was coming through it, however, so he judged it to be some sort of a ventilator.

The walls, it was a square room, were made of rough pine board, supported every few feet by solid six-by-six uprights. The ceiling, too, was beamed. There was a single door to his left.

Stationed at the door, was a tough-looking character in the uniform of a Black Invader. Across the table from him, smiling his infectious smile, was Zytoff. The man gestured toward the food.

"I guess we're both pretty hungry, captain, eh? Shall we eat first and talk later?"

Unconsciously Dusty was sliding his hand toward his holstered automatic. He, himself, only realized the movement when he found that his gun had been taken away. At that moment, Zytoff, too, saw and understood the movement.

"Naturally, I couldn't let you keep it, captain," he said in a soft, chiding voice. "You should be satisfied that I've left your hands free to eat with."

"Thanks," Dusty grunted, and let his eyes glide over toward the door.

Zytoff's next remark almost proved him a perfect mind reader in Dusty's opinion.

"Yes, he's armed, and an excellent shot, captain. So is the other soldier on the other side of that door. And, myself, too, if you'll permit me to say so. Look—see that knot in that board over there—to your right?"

Dusty snapped his eyes around, saw the knot, frowned back at Zytoff.

"Watch, captain, if you will."

THE BLACK was leaning both elbows on the edge of the table. Suddenly he became a whirlwind of motion. No, rather he became a human bolt of lightning. Down went his right hand, up it came in almost the same split second.

There was a gun in his grip and it crashed out sound. Impulsively Dusty glanced toward the knot. There was a neat hole the fraction of an inch from the dead center. He turned back toward Zytoff and grinned.

"Not bad," he said. "I guess I'll eat!"

"My compliments on your sane decision," murmured Zytoff.

"I'm sure you'll find a Black Invader repast quite as delicious as your own American food."

The man spoke the truth. That, Dusty was forced to admit to himself after the first mouthful of food. True, he was as hungry as a starved wolf. But regardless of that, he could think of few places where he'd ever tasted anything better.

By the time he was halfway finished, he had forgotten the dull ache in his head; almost forgotten the seriousness of his predicament. In short, he was fast becoming a new man again.

However, as they both finished the meal, Zytoff brought him right smack back to the situation at hand.

"And now, captain, I suppose you are wondering more than ever just why I've brought you here? But first—a cigarette?"

The Black pushed a box across the table. Dusty took one and lighted up.

"I guess so," he nodded, spewing smoke ceilingward. "But where's here?"

The other waved his hand airily.

"Sorry, but that's my little secret," he said. "But to get to other things. You're here for two reasons. One, so that I may get to know you real well. Your record has always fascinated me, you know. And second, to try and discover just how much your friends know."

Dusty puffed placidly on his cigarette a moment. Then said, "As to the first, lots of folks don't consider me a nice fellow to know. I scare small children. Make them run home screaming to their mothers and have horrible nightmares. And for the second reason, well, ask me any questions about the Yank forces.

I'll be tickled to death to tell you. Tell you what—I'll even draw a map of some of our most important fortifications. Got a pencil and some paper?"

Zytoff smiled and nodded his head patiently.

"I was hoping that you'd volunteer all that information," he said lightly. "I knew I could count on you. You're so obliging. As a matter of fact, the outer defenses of New York harbor have always intrigued me."

"Oh, those?" scoffed Dusty. "That will be simple. I designed and planned them myself, you know. Why, one day I was saying to the President—and a few big shots of the war department—gentlemen, here is what we should do regarding New York harbor. First, we'll have to—"

"Splendid!" Zytoff clapped his hands and stood up. "At last I'm going to find out! But never mind the details, captain. Tell you what—get it all pictured in your mind, and be ready to tell me when I get back. Sorry, but I've got something else to do just now. You'll excuse me?"

"Sure," Dusty grinned. "Mind if I walk about the place? First time I've been here, you know."

The Black showed all of his teeth in a loud laugh.

"If we both survive the war," he said, "which we probably won't, I shall insist that we team up in vaudeville, or perhaps television. Sorry, you'll have to remain here, captain. I've got to prepare for your friends arriving—if they do arrive."

That brought Dusty up straight.

"What?"

Zytoff, at the door, gestured.

"Why, captain!" he said in a mimicked voice of surprise, "how could I find out how much your friends know unless I asked them? Ta-ta, see you soon. But, oh yes, a tip. The guard here is a far better shot even than I am. A point to remember, captain!"

With a smile and a short nod, Zytoff jerked open the door, stepped through, and closed it quickly behind him. Not knowing just what to think at the moment, Dusty lighted another cigarette and sank slowly down into his chair. Then, chin braced on one fist, he sat scowling darkly at the opposite wall.

For several minutes, the cigarette burned unnoticed between his fingers. Then it burned him and he smudged it out with a muttered curse. In a way, though, the burn was of some help. It jarred him out of a foggy trance, and thoughts began coming to him in a somewhat logical sequence.

To begin with, Curly and Biff were undoubtedly safe. They had not come close enough for the Metal-Meltic to catch them. Metal-Meltic? Yeah, that's the stuff Zytoff must have used—though he didn't say so in so many words. The Yanks think up something for ground use, and the Blacks swipe it and use it in the air! Hell—what a war!

But to get back to himself. Let's see, why was he here and where was he? The last, he didn't know exactly. Some place near the Rockies, he guessed. And why had Zytoff allowed him to live? Nuts! What did the guy mean—"to try and discover how much your friends know"? What friends? Curly and Jack?

"By God, does he think they'll follow me here?"

As he shouted the words aloud he stood up straight. The

guard at the door, instantly swung up his gun and trained it on Dusty's chest.

"You will take care, American!"

The words came from the Black's throat as though he had trouble in dragging them out. Dusty gave him but a snap side glance, slumped back in the chair, brain racing madly at top speed.

Curly and Jack follow him here? Here? Where? Was some ship tagging their tail—tagging the tail of Zytoff's crate? No. It couldn't be that. Curly and Biff would have sprung something before now. Now? What time was it, anyway?

He glanced at his wrist watch, noticed for the first time that the crystal guard had been crushed inward, cracking the crystal and jamming the hands on the dial. It had happened at sixteen minutes of two. He turned his head toward the guard.

"Hey, you! What's the time?"

A wide, stained-tooth grin and a shrug was his only answer. Dusty let it pass, fell to brooding at the opposite wall again. If only he knew what the hell it was all about, then he might think up some line of action.

Damn Zytoff, anyway! The bum was playing him for a fare-thee-well. A darn queer type to be a Black Invader, though. Certainly acted like a white man. At least, as white as a member of the enemy could be.

That crack about Morgan got him, though. He hadn't expected that. But had it made any lasting effect on him? Guess not. Since that first mention, the Black hadn't spoken of Metal-Meltic or the formula again. Either he wasn't interested or else he was one damn clever egg playing a damn clever game. AS THE minutes dragged on, and further concentrated thought resulted in getting him exactly nowhere, he heaved up out of his chair, and with hands jammed in his pockets started ambling about the room. His getting up put the guard instantly on the alert.

The man's gun hand became rigid, only the muzzle of the gun moving as Dusty changed position. Out the corner of his eye, the Yank noticed the seemingly awkward way the Black handled the gun. When he moved it to the right his forefinger seemed hardly to be touching the trigger.

That apparent fact, plus curiosity and wild imagination seething up in Dusty, resulted in a grim, yet insane decision. Puckering his lips he whistled softly to himself, continued strolling around and around the room, eyes bent on the floor. But on each circuit he drew a few inches nearer to the Black.

"You try tricks—I shoot, American!"

The dragged out words smote Dusty's ears as he was making what he had decided would be the last circuit. Once more around and he would try his luck. Like hell, he would now!

He stopped, looked blankly at the guard.

"Huh? What did you say?"

"You try tricks and I shoot!" growled the man. "I hear lots about you. You will not fool me, no!"

Dusty laughed, kicked at an imaginary stone on the floor, and casually swung back toward the guard.

"Do you think I'm crazy?" he exclaimed. "I saw your boss

shoot, didn't I? Well, he says that you're even better. Tricks? Yeah, I look like I got a bag full of them don't I!"

The guard's thick lips twitched back in what could have been a grimace or a smile. But he took neither his eyes nor the muzzle of his gun off Dusty for one single split second.

"That is good then!" he rumbled. "You had better not try those tricks!"

"Not today," said Dusty. Then with a grin, "But I'll tell you something. I bet I could grab that gun away from you with my bare hands, before you could kill me. And what do you think of that?"

As Dusty spoke he moved casually toward the guard's right. The Black immediately followed him around with the muzzle of the gun—and made no comment.

Dusty moved his hands in his pockets.

"With these two hands, right here in my pockets," he grinned. "Grab your gun away, and you wouldn't kill me. Know why? Well, I'll tell you. Because it's my hunch that the big boss would wring your pretty neck if you killed me. Your orders are not to shoot to kill, are they?"

The guard shrugged, muttered.

"You play no tricks on me, American!"

"Just what I thought," nodded Dusty, shifting his weight to his left foot. "Oh, you'd shoot, but not to kill. That's why I could get my hands out, and grab that gun before you'd dare pull the trigger! Want to see me do it?"

The guard's eyes narrowed and his lips went back.

"You will try no—"

100

"Save it!" Dusty cut in. "Don't worry, I'm not going to!"

He gave the Black a scornful look, puckered his lips to whistle, and started to turn away. It was at that instant he saw the guard relax a bit, take his eyes from his hands buried in his pockets. And it was during that very instant that Dusty whipped into action with the speed of a striking cobra.

Hands still jammed in his pockets, he swung his right foot across his left leg and up. No human eye could have followed that movement, and the Black guard was no exception. Perhaps he sensed it, however, for a wild light leaped into his jet-black eyes. Too late, though, his brain grasped the full significance of what was taking place.

Before he could even begin to crook his trigger finger, the toe of Dusty's boot crashed into his wrist. There was a sharp crack of bones breaking, and the gun went flying across the room.

In what was practically a continuation of the whole general movement, Dusty's clenched right fist whipped out of his pocket, and arced upward with every ounce of his one hundred and eighty-five pounds behind it.

A cry, rising up from the guard's throat, died before it was even given life. Like a tree trunk that has been sawed in two the Black fell over sidewise, stiff and rigid, and totally unconscious. Flinging out his other hand, the Yank caught him, eased him down and pulled him away from the door.

"Next time you'll remember that people have feet as well as hands!" he muttered at the still figure. "Figured that the hand angle would hold your attention."

Turning swiftly away, he crossed the room, picked up the guard's gun, and then tiptoed back to the door. Ear pressed against it, he listened intently for a moment. There was no sound on the other side. He scowled, reached for the knob, but changed his mind and jerked his hand away.

A moment or two longer, he hesitated. Then with an inward curse, he grasped the door knob again, slowly applied pressure, and began to twist, the fraction of an inch at a time. Bit by bit, bit by bit, until the knob would not turn any more.

Gun clenched in his left hand, he eased the door open, eased it open so slowly that in a crazy, excitement-inspired sort of way his brain told him that the door wasn't moving at all!

PERHAPS IT was seconds, perhaps hours: at any rate, to his tingling nerves it seemed an eternity before there was a crack big enough for him to peer through. And when he did, he saw the broad shoulders of another Black guard, not two feet away, standing back to him.

Dusty grinned. Just what the doctor ordered! Damned if it wasn't going to be round two for the poor people!

Silently he eased the door open another inch or two; just enough to slip his gun hand through. His eyes were riveted on the point in the small of the Black's back, where he would jam the muzzle of the gun.

That would be better than trying to clout the bum. He might miss, or because of his unbalanced position, might not hit hard enough. Plenty of time to smack him later. Ramming the gun muzzle into the man's back would be plenty for the moment.

Tight-lipped, body tensed, Dusty moved the gun forward—

and stopped it a couple of inches from the man's back. The sound of footsteps coming down the stairs, at the end of the twenty foot corridor, smacked against his ear-drums. The Black stiffened to attention. Over his shoulder, Dusty caught the flash glance of shiny black-booted feet, then coarse, baggy-knee breeches and then a skin-tight tunic with a pair of gold wings— and then the lower part of a face.

Zytoff was coming back!

For one infinitesimal iota of time, Dusty crouched paralyzed. His gun was still a couple of inches from the Black guard. He could cower the man, perhaps, use him as a shield against Zytoff, and trust to luck from then on. No, it wasn't worth the risk. Better let Zytoff come inside—then get him!

Ducking down so that the Black guard hid him completely from the approaching Zytoff, Dusty pulled his gun hand back, twisted sidewise and pushed the door shut.

With as much speed as he dared, he turned the knob back and allowed the latch to catch. Then stepping to the side, he flattened himself against the wall, switched his gun to his right hand, and waited breathlessly.

The seconds slipped by. He thought he heard the sound of voices beyond the door, but he wasn't sure. Hell, maybe he was wrong. Maybe Zytoff was coming to the room. Had he seen another door leading off the corridor outside? He couldn't remember. He'd concentrated on the guard's back. And then the approach of Zytoff had grabbed his attention.

Maybe there was a door. Maybe Zytoff had gone through it. If so, swell! He'd try the outside guard again. And—

The sharp rapping of knuckles against the other side of the door stopped his wandering thoughts. He held his breath; didn't move a single muscle. Then came a voice—the clear, pleasant voice of Zytoff, with just an echo of patient chiding in it.

"Captain Ayres! Why be so foolish? Open the door, and toss that gun out. It is not going to help you in the slightest! I know you've taken it away from the guard, you see?"

The man's words banged and slammed around inside Dusty's head. One split second he was boiling with rage, and the next he felt like a five-year-old who has been caught with his hand in the jam jar. Zytoff knew? What the hell—and how the hell? He gripped the gun tighter, made not a sound. There was a pause of a moment or so, and then Zytoff's voice came through the door again.

"Be sensible, captain! Don't you realize that you're trapped? Just toss the gun out here, and it will save us a lot of trouble. Be sane, captain. You are completely helpless!"

Dusty's jaws squared, and his eyes became hard.

"Yeah?" he barked through the door. "Why not appoint yourself a committee of one, and come in and get it? I'll even let you get the door open. Maybe let you have first shot."

A low chuckle came back to tighten his nerves all the more.

"A contest of that sort can wait until another time, captain! I'm asking you for the last time—will you toss your gun outside and surrender like a sensible person? The sensible person I've always understood you to be?"

As though the other were in the room with him, Dusty shook his head doggedly.

"I like this gun!" he grated. "And I'm keeping it!"

Silence for a moment. Silence, heavy and sombre. Then, from beyond the door.

"Very well, captain—if you wish it that way!"

"I do! And that's flat! You can have this damn gun when you come and get it!"

Whether his action was insane or not, Dusty didn't even give it a thought. He was trapped between four walls. Zytoff could wait him out, even try to starve him into submission. Maybe and maybe not. He had a gun in his hand, and there were death slugs in that gun. Let there be a show-down! Damn right, a show-down. And the sooner it came, the—

An eerie weakness rippled through his body. His eyes began to water, his chest to burn—and there was a strange giddiness in his head. He found himself straining every ounce of his strength to hold the gun up. Sweat broke out of his forehead, and a great invisible weight dragged down on his shoulders.

Damn! What the devil was the matter with him? He was down on one knee. He couldn't get up. He was being pushed down, pushed down flat on the floor. There didn't seem to be any air in the room.

His lungs were sucking in fire. Hell—keep the gun up—keep the gun up! The spell will pass. Just a relapse, maybe, from that crack on the head. Damn you, you can't pass out now. Passing out like a baby? Can't take it, by God! A little smack on the head is getting you down!

Then through blurred eyes he saw the filmy, milk-white wisps seeping into the room through the ventilator opening, or whatever the hell it was. Gas! The bums were gassing him! Snuffing him out like a damn rat in a trap!

"Damn you! Damn the whole blasted lot of you!"

From out of a swirling, ringing fog he heard his own hoarse voice. Then there was a crash of sound, another, and another. He saw flame spurting from the muzzle of the gun in his right hand, saw that it was pointed up toward the opening in the wall.

Yet he couldn't feel it between his fingers, couldn't even feel that he was pulling the trigger. He was, however. The crash of sound, and the flame spurting from the muzzle proved it.

A defiant laugh echoed back to him. It came from his own lips. He was laughing. Damn right! He'd show the bums! He'd lay every slug right through that opening, and pick off the tramp beyond. Gas him, would they? He'd show 'em! No—no—put a couple through the door! It wasn't very thick. Maybe Zytoff was still out there waiting!

Sure! A couple through the door. Might get the big stiff. Serve him right. Get the big stiff—just—for—luck!

His hand wouldn't move! The gun had ceased firing. He wasn't even pulling the trigger. He—and then with a thunderous roar of sound the walls of the room caved in and the ceiling crashed down on top of him!

CHAPTER 9
EAGLE TRAP

PITCH-BLACK DARKNESS slowly fading away; tiny shreds of faint light piercing through it, becoming brighter and brighter. The shreds of light merged together, and became a solid glow that drove the darkness farther and farther away.

Through dazed and blinking eyes, Dusty dully became conscious of the fact that he was staring at pine boards fitted together and braced by heavy beams.

Steeling himself against the spinning merry-go-round in his head, he forced himself up to a sitting position, pressed the tips of his fingers hard against his temples and concentrated on focusing his eyes on his blurred surroundings.

Gradually the filmy mist cleared from his eyes, and he found himself in an entirely different room. It was much smaller than the other. It contained a cot on which he sat, a couple of chairs, and a knocked-together table. On the table was a glass and a bottle. There was a brandy label on the bottle, and more important, dark amber liquid in the bottle.

He stared at it a moment while strength flowed back into his veins, then pushed himself up and lunged across the few feet of floor space to the table. Snapping off the bottle cap he sniffed the contents. It was real brandy—smelled every bit as mellow as some he had had from a flask, Zytoff's flask.

Tipping the bottle he splashed some into the glass, took a sip. It tasted the same, too. And in one gulp he downed a man-sized shot, lurched back to the cot and sat down. Head buried in his hands he waited for the tingling warmth to spread to all parts of his body.

It not only did that, but banished the few remaining cobwebs in his brain. When he eventually raised his head and surveyed the room again, the objects in it were no longer blurred, nor did they make any attempt to dance around before his gaze.

"If my dome didn't still ache," he grunted aloud, "I'd say that this whole damn business was one grand, cockeyed nightmare."

The sound of his own voice brought a queer sense of comfort to him. It seemed to make his heart pump the blood faster through his veins, filled him with a renewed sense of vigor—and curiosity. It was the last that forced him to his feet again, and started him on a tour of inspection.

The tour was short, very short indeed. As a matter of fact, right straight over to the door that he suddenly noticed on the opposite side of the room. As he reached it he paused, and like once before, pressed his ear against the wood, listening intently. But as before, he could not hear the slightest sound on the other side.

Straightening up, he chewed his lip in scowling silence a moment, then shrugged and boldly grasped the knob and twisted. He half expected to find that the door was locked, or at least hear movement on the other side—the quick shifting of feet, the growl of a Black guard on the alert. But to his amazement the door swung inward at his tug, and he found himself gaping into another room, little different from the one in which he woke up.

He swept it with puzzled eyes, stiffened, and let out a sharp cry. On the cot to his left was the figure of a man half bundled up in flying clothes. The flying clothes were of the U.S. Air Force type. The man's head was half buried in the fur collar, hiding his face.

In two wild leaps, Dusty reached the side of the cot. He reached down and pushed back the fur collar to look at the face.

"Curly! My God, Curly!"

His booming shout echoed and reechoed about the room as he stood gazing down into the pale still features of his pal. For a moment he couldn't believe his eyes. He cursed, roughly brushed the back of his hand across them, and looked again. The unconscious figure was still that of Curly Brooks.

Spinning, Dusty tore back into the other room, snatched up the brandy bottle and glass, and came racing back. Pausing long enough to pour some into the glass, he then sat on the edge of the cot, hoisted Curly's head and shoulders with his left hand, and forced some of the brandy between the pale twisted lips.

Just a few drops. A wait of a few seconds, then another few drops.

BY THAT time the first few drops had trickled down Brooks' throat. His body twitched, and he coughed violently. Dusty held his nose, forcing him to swallow it all. Weakly, Curly's hands came up, tried to push himself away from Dusty's grasp. Then, presently, the lean pilot's eyes fluttered open. Blank orbs stared up at Dusty. They cleared a bit, and the faint light of recognition seeped into them.

Dusty heaved a long thankful sigh, grinned.

DUSTY
AYRES

"Yup!" he nodded. "It's yours truly."

Curly blinked a few more times, but didn't speak. With Dusty's help he worked himself up to a sitting position, rubbed his hand across the left side of his head, and groaned. Dusty saw the goose-egg and the blood-matted hair on the top of it.

"Take your hand down, kid," he said. "Here, let me look at it."

"Just a bump," Curly mumbled thickly, still rubbing. "Got clouted by a Black and—"

Brooks dropped his hand, turned toward Dusty.

"Say, what's the big idea?" he yelled with surprising energy. "How come you sent a Black receiving party to meet me? You damn fool, I followed your instructions, and damn near got killed!"

"Hey, hold it!" Dusty cut in. "What are you raving about? I didn't give you any instructions? I—o-o-oh, you mean about you and Biff tailing me? But, where's—"

"Biff and me tailing you, hell!" Curly snarled. "I mean about you contacting me on the radio—telling me to land on that damn ledge. Well, I did, and three Blacks jumped me. Hell, one of their slugs just grazed my chest! It glanced off the buckle of my Sam Browne and knocked me kicking! Then they came down on me like three ton of bricks. The lights went out! And here I am. Now, what—"

"Hold it some more!" Dusty barked, and held out the brand glass. "Here, take another swallow. You're still out of your nut!"

Curly took a swallow, coughed over it and glared at his best friend.

"Out of my nut, am I?" he yelled, the blood rushing back to his cheeks. "Say! What is this, anyway?"

"Somebody's crazy," said Dusty. "And I feel all right. What do you mean, I gave you radio instructions to land on a ledge? What ledge—where?"

A puzzled look drove the anger from Curly's eyes. He stared hard at Dusty, started to speak a couple of times, but couldn't seem to find words. Dusty watched him anxiously, his eyes traveling unconsciously to the goose egg on Curly's head.

"You didn't get me on the radio?" Brooks finally questioned in a vacant tone. "Didn't tell me to land on that ledge—that snow-packed ledge between the third and fourth peak?"

"Of course I didn't, kid!" Dusty said in quick reply. "You've been having bad dreams. But how the hell did you get here?"

"Yeah, bad dreams!" murmured Curly thickly. Then, "Huh? Bad dreams, my eye! How'd I get here? On a tip from Jack. Came in your ship. You saw me, in the glasses. You contacted me. You told me where to land. You told me to wait. Then, wham-o—those tramps jumped me. That's how I got here! Now, how about telling me a few of the answers? Or haven't I been initiated enough yet?"

Dusty laid a hand on his arm.

"Pull up, kid, pull up!" he soothed. "Something's screwy—very screwy!"

"I'll say!" Brooks growled. "Next time why not add Fire-Eyes to your welcoming committee?"

"For God's sake, pipe down!" Dusty snapped. "You're talking in circles. Hell, man, I didn't do any of the things you say I did.

I've been a prisoner ever since I went down. I was shanghaied—shanghaied by none other than Zytoff."

Dusty went on to tell in rapid sentences of his experience.

"And when I came out of it, and came into this room, I find you," he finished up.

Curly muttered a groan, went back to rubbing his head.

"It doesn't make sense!" he grunted. "I've heard your voice enough to be able to recognize it. It was you all right—but maybe it wasn't. Nuts and more nuts!"

Dusty scowled at the floor a few moments, then took hold of Curly's hand and pulled it away from his head.

"Listen, Curly," he began, "we've got to try and match things together—make something out of it all. Let's hear your story from the time I was attacked."

Brooks took time out to have another swallow of brandy. Then, clearing his throat, he told his story from beginning to end.

"At least it all checks with Jack's hunch," he grunted at the end. "While we've been sitting by the fire knitting, the Blacks have entrenched themselves—right in our own back yard, by God! Zytoff? You're sure it's Zytoff?"

Dusty shrugged.

"He said he was! And there's no reason to disbelieve him. But you say that Crandall died without leaving the real formula? Damn! The hell with that, now, though. A side issue, for the present. The point is the jam we're both in now. You shouldn't have come alone, Curly. Jack was right—should have organized a regular searching party."

"And it would probably have searched until hell froze over before it found this place!" Brooks bit off. "Our big question is where do we go from here?"

"We go no place, Curly, old kid!"

The two of them sat up straight. Curly gaped wide-eyed at Dusty, "Your—your voice!" he choked out. "But but you didn't say anything. You didn't even open your mouth!"

Dusty hardly heard him. Speak? He knew damn well that he hadn't spoken. But he, too, had heard a voice say, "We go no place, Curly, old kid!" A voice that was such a dead-ringer for his own, that for split seconds he wondered if he really was mistaken—if he really had spoken.

AND THEN from in back of him, he heard a soft chuckle. Whirling, he saw Zytoff standing in the open doorway between the two rooms. The Black had a mile-wide grin on his good looking face, and his eyes were fairly dancing with merriment. In his right hand, however, was a very business-like looking Invader gas pistol.

Still grinning, Zytoff advanced a step or two into the room.

"Vanity prevents me from keeping it a secret any longer," he said. "Yes, the art of imitating human voices has been one of my very few accomplishments, since childhood. It was I who deceived you, Lieutenant Brooks. But pleading the necessities of waging war, I state that I could do nothing else. You'll forgive me?"

Curly fixed him with a hard eye.

"Sure!" he grated. "Think nothing of it. You must do it for the wife and kiddies sometime!"

Zytoff arched his eyebrows, switching his gaze to Dusty's scowling face.

"And you, captain," he said, "you've learned your lesson, I hope? You certainly seem to enjoy forcing people to kill you. It could have been other than paralytic gas, you know."

Dust said nothing. Hands locked on his crossed knees, he simply stared steadily at the Black. There wasn't much else he could do. It was entirely Zytoff's party, and to all indications it would continue to be his party. On impulse, Dusty put his thought into words.

"What do we play at next?" he bit off.

The Black shrugged, made a waving motion with the gas pistol in his hand.

"I really haven't made up my mind on that point," he said. "You see, you have served your purpose—both of you—and frankly, I don't know if there are any other games we could play."

Curly stumbled to his feet, bunched his fists.

"Park that gas gun!" he growled, "and I'll play smack-ing-the-kisser with you—if you've got the nerve!"

"Skip it, kid!" Dusty barked, dragging him down on the cot. "General Baccalaureate here has got a lot more words on his chest. Okay, you, how come we've served our purpose? Got us all fixed for your private zoo, or something?"

"That's an idea," nodded the other smiling. "But I wonder how your memory is, captain? Remember speaking about Morgan and the new Metal-Meltic formula? Well, I guess there isn't any new formula, is there? Didn't Lieutenant Brooks just say so? But something a bit more important to me just now—Lieutenant Horner's men have got suspicious about this region in the Rockies, eh? That, my friend, was what I really did want to know!"

Zytoff paused long enough to lick his lips, then went on.

"That was what I meant when I said that I brought you here in order to find out what your friends knew. And now that I have found out—and can take steps to throw off further discovery—both of you cease to be of very much use to me.

"However, Lieutenant Brooks, I want you to know that I admire your courage and your sense of friendship for Captain Ayres. It's a pity that it led you to such disastrous results.

"You see, had you made no attempt to find the captain out here, I would have become convinced that our little secret hiding place was secret. Now I am forewarned, and yes, exceedingly forearmed!"

Had not Dusty kept a tight hold on Curly's arm, the lean pilot would have leaped to his feet and blindly flung himself at the grinning Black just inside the room. But Dusty jerked him back and gave his arm a meaning squeeze. With a muttered curse, Curly relaxed and sat clenching and unclenching his fists.

"Okay," Dusty nodded at Zytoff. "I guess you win the first couple of rounds. But that isn't the whole fight, not by a damn sight. I don't know what kind of a layout you got here. And personally I don't give a damn. But it won't be worth a hoot in hell to you. And that's fact!

"Brooks came after me but there are ten or fifteen thousand winged hard guys that will come after him. There's a couple of others who know just about where he is, and you can bet your sweet life they're not going to go to sleep on it. So pack up and drift, Zytoff. I almost like you—that is, for an enemy—so take my tip, pack up and drift while you can!"

The Black bowed stiffly from the waist.

"Thank you, captain," he said. "But I don't think I will take your advice, you see, having heard you and Lieutenant Brooks compare notes. In this manner, incidentally."

Zytoff cut himself off short, moved over to the far wall. Reaching out his free hand, he moved a panel so cleverly hidden in the wall that to all appearances it looked like a part of the wall itself. In back of the panel, however, Dusty saw the receiving disc of a dictograph. Sight of it sent the blood to his cheeks, and in helpless rage he glanced at Curly Brooks. An expression of bitter chagrin was stamped on his pal's face.

"As I was saying," suddenly came Zytoff's words, "having heard you and the lieutenant compare notes, I know exactly what to expect—and exactly what to do. No one knows where you are, captain. No one knows exactly, I mean.

"There are, however, one or two who have an idea where Lieutenant Brooks might be. For that reason it would be impractical for me to detain him here much longer. In other words, I believe that I shall return the lieutenant to his friends. And keep you for—shall we say, good measure?"

Dusty nodded grimly.

"Okay, with me," he grunted. "But you're going to be in for a big surprise, Zytoff!"

"Yes?"

117

"Yes! Brooks will come back with the others and knock the hell out of this place. I'm telling him to do that right now!"

The Black smiled.

"Tell him anything you wish, captain," he said. "But it will do neither you nor him any good. When Lieutenant Brooks returns to his friends, he will not be able to remember where he has been. And if the miracle happens—if he should remember—he will remember what I say right now.

"The first American plane that we sight near this particular spot will be our signal to kill you, Captain Ayres! And I promise you that it shall be done!"

Hardly had the man finished when there echoed out of the distance the crash of rifle fire.

CHAPTER 10
K.O. TWINS

AS ONE man, both Dusty and Curly leaped to their feet and stood rigid. Zytoff, however, didn't move; didn't even bat an eyelash. Then he slowly smiled.

"Don't raise your hopes, gentlemen," he said quietly. "Those shots do not mean we are being attacked. On the contrary, they mean that my men have settled a little problem according to their own judgment."

Half turning, the Black snapped something through the open door in his native tongue. As though by magic, three burly Invader soldiers appeared, and in less than half a minute Dusty and Curly had their wrists bound tightly behind their backs.

Zytoff took a couple of seconds to examine the job, seemed satisfied and motioned toward the door leading into the room where Dusty woke up.

"Walk in there," he ordered. "And if you are wise, make no foolish moves. I'll not resort to paralysis gas next time, captain."

Heart like a lump of lead, Dusty led the way into the other room. Stepping quickly around him, one of the guards moved over to the other door and jerked it open. It opened into a long corridor, dimly lighted. Zytoff nodded him through, behind the guard.

Along the corridor went the entire party, marching up a short flight of steps at the far end. At the top, the procession turned left, and finally went through another door that led into a large dome-shaped room.

At first, Dusty glanced around him casually. He was too troubled with his spinning thoughts to care much about where they were going. But suddenly, he stopped short and a sharp gasp escaped his lips.

The walls of the room were lined with airplane parts. There were at least fifty dismantled engines, countless wing sections and fuselages, glass cockpits cowlings, struts, tail sections, and everything else that goes into the complete airplane. In other words, the room was a well equipped airplane assembly depot.

"Interesting, isn't it?"

Dusty unconsciously turned to stare into Zytoff's grinning face. The Black made a waving motion with his hand.

"Now you see, captain, why I do not care to take your advice and drift, as you put it? My plans have gone too far for me to abandon them now."

Though the man had not said so in as many words, Dusty knew the meaning of it all. Right here in the heart of America, Zytoff had established a perfect secret air base. The task of

CURLY BROOKS

burrowing into the Rockies seemed almost unbelievable of accomplishment. But—there about the room was proof that the unbelievable had been accomplished.

And at about the same instant, Dusty saw the mobile airplane catapult by the wall to his left. Zytoff, following his gaze, grinned and nodded his head.

"Taking off from the ledge outside might be noticed," he said. "So we will catapult from inside the mountain. Look—what do you think of this little invention?"

The Black moved over to a row of levers, such as one sees in the switch house of a large railroad yard. He pulled one back, and there was instantly the whir of hidden gear wheels. And to Dusty's utter amazement the forward wall split into two pieces. Half of it lowered down into the floor, and the other half moved up into the ceiling.

Cold air rushed into the room. But Dusty hardly felt the change. Rooted to the spot, he stood gaping into the room beyond. It was a smaller room—more like a cave, as matter of fact, for there was no front side. It opened out onto a tree-fringed, snow-packed ledge.

Yet so cleverly placed was the opening that even though one was on the ledge the opening could not be seen behind the trees. They were a perfect shield, and permitted entrance to the cave-like room on the right side. There the trees had been removed, leaving an opening just big enough for an airplane to pass through.

All that, Dusty saw and realized in a couple of seconds. And then he saw something that made the blood pound against his temples. In the outer room, not over twenty-five yards from where he stood, was the Silver Flash.

The Flash! Seeing it there, hemmed in like a caged eagle, was almost more than he could stand. A savage curse rushed off his lips, and he would have moved toward it, had not one of the guards grabbed him and jerked him back. Zytoff laughed in his face.

"Sorry, captain," he chuckled. "But I guess that it is my plane now. I don't think that you'll be needing it any more. Rather an attractive show-piece in a museum, don't you think?"

Dusty didn't answer. He was too choked up to say anything. Though Curly had told him about landing, only now did he fully realize that the Flash was here in this damn place. It was almost as much of a jolt as finding Curly Brooks.

Then, he saw something else—another plane beyond the Silver Flash. It was a big, all-red monoplane pursuit. And as he looked at it, he knew instinctively that it was the plane in which Zytoff had kidnaped him.

One thing in particular caught his attention and held it. Just back of the cockpit were two tanks built into the top of the fuselage. From each tank a pipe ran back the full length of the fuselage, up the fin to the top of the rudder where it flanged out.

Instantly, there appeared in Dusty's brain a picture of blue hell spewing out across night-darkened skies, and once again he felt terrific heat—terrific heat that seemed to sear him from head to foot. He also thought of the three valve knobs he had seen at the rear of the cockpit.

"A crude arrangement, I'll have to admit," Zytoff's voice broke in on his thoughts. "But in the time allowed I think I did a rather good job of it. A shame that Major Crandall did not leave either of us the complete formula. I shall have to go sparingly with what there is left in the tanks. That is, until my own engineers and chemists work out a new formula. By the way, they tell me that it will not be difficult."

Though he felt far from it, Dusty forced a grin on his lips.

"Yeah?" he snorted. "And what do you think we'll be doing in the meantime?"

Zytoff shrugged.

"Working on it too, I suppose," he said quietly. "But even if you are successful, too, we will still have the advantage, I'm afraid. Yes, with this perfect starting point for raids, once the snow goes we will be able to inflict considerable damage from within. You follow me?"

DUSTY DID, and only too well. Secretly entrenched as Zytoff and his gang were, they could smash into the very vitals of the U.S. and get away with it, too. The Metal-Meltic angle was only a small part of the man's general plan of operation. By good fortune he had stumbled upon it and would make use of it only because it happened to fit in with the general scheme of things.

A secret air base, right here in the very heart of the Rockies! The thought slammed and banged around inside Dusty's brain, as he stood gazing helplessly about. The Black Hawk had been a clever devil. Ekar had been even more clever. But neither of them could hold a candle to the smooth cunning of this one— of Zytoff. What hellish plans lay behind those twinkling eyes of his, only God knew.

At that moment a group of Black Invader pilots, carrying a limp figure between them, entered in at the right corner of the other room. Marching to the rear they dumped their burden on the floor, and then one of them came up to Zytoff, saluted and spoke rapidly in his native tongue.

Zytoff answered with a short nod, and turned to Dusty and Curly.

"They fired those shots you heard," he smiled. "One of my men became just a little bit too ambitious. He took off in my plane, there, late yesterday afternoon. True, he claimed that he destroyed an American plane with the Metal-Meltic. But one plane is too costly. Rather than pass judgment on him myself, I allowed my men to act as the court. They—they pronounced the death sentence on him. And he has paid for his unwarranted ambition."

"Corbin, of the Twentieth! The one whose S.O.S. I picked up!"

Dusty hardly heard the sharp cry from Curly's lips. His complete attention was riveted on Zytoff, and for the first time he was beginning to realize the sense of utter ruthlessness in the man's make-up. The grinning lips, the twinkling eyes, and the pleasant mannerism all went to cover up the deadly inner nature of the man.

To gain his end Zytoff would go to all limits, regardless. Hell yes, only such a man as he could have engineered the establishing of this secret air base—right in the heart of enemy country. Cunning, fearless, and deadly beyond words to describe.

"And I was beginning to almost consider you a white man!" Dusty grated at him. "I should have known better!"

The Black took it without a single show of anger.

"You should have known better in reference to many things," he replied evenly. "I believe in getting things done. Mercy and consideration are only a means toward the fulfillment of what you wish to accomplish. And now—"

There was a wild shout at the far end of the room. A door slammed open and a thin, iron-gray haired little man came dashing through it. He was waving strained hands crazily about, and shrill sounds were pouring out of a cadaverous looking mouth. For a second he pulled up short, then seeing Zytoff, he came scuttling over, still waving both hands and still shrilling at the top of his voice.

Whatever he was saying had a tremendous effect upon Zytoff, for he clapped the man on the back, and spoke to him in what sounded to Dusty as a tone of wild praise. Then giving the man a push, he sent him scuttling back across the room again, and turned beaming eyes on the two Yanks.

"Good news, gentlemen!" he exclaimed. "That was my chief chemist. He came to tell me that he and his associates have worked out the formula, and that no part of it is any longer a secret. I am so pleased that I believe I'll let you see for yourselves. Neither of you would benefit by it anyway."

A nod at the waiting guards put them to work. They immediately took hold of Dusty and Curly and marched them forward in the wake of Zytoff who was already striding toward the door through which the chemist had disappeared.

Sick at heart, unable to collect his thoughts, Dusty allowed the guard to shove him forward without any resistance. Like a man going to his doom, he stumbled through the doorway and down a short corridor to a door at the far end.

The door was open, and through it he saw a well-appointed chemical laboratory. Zytoff was already in the room and in excited conversation with three other figures, one of whom was the little old man. They were bending over two small tanks with a petcock opening at one end. Two feet away, in a stone tray, was a small pile of junk metal—scraps of dural, brass, and steel and iron.

For a few seconds the little old man talked and gesticulated with his hands. Then motioning the others back, he reached out and twisted the petcocks the fraction of a hair.

Instantly there was a sort of whistling hissing sound, and from out of each petcock came a tiny thread of blue gas. At a point a couple of inches from the pile of metal the two blue threads mingled with each other, and became a sort of shimmering blue spray that slithered down over the metal.

The transformation that took place on that stone tray was almost instantaneous. Like a lump of butter struck by the flame of a blow torch, the dural, brass, steel, and iron scraps shriveled up and became a discolored pool that smoked and sputtered. With a wild cry, the little old man shut off both petcocks and turned triumphant eyes on Zytoff.

The Black commander nodded his enthusiasm, and into his face came a look that turned Dusty's heart to a lump of ice. It was the look of a man gone completely mad with triumph—and for the moment completely stripped of all humane traits and characteristics.

But the look was gone in almost no time, and when Zytoff turned toward Dusty. His expression had returned to normal.

"You see?" he said, nodding toward the hissing pool of molten metal. "You see what we have accomplished?"

Dusty said nothing, nor did Curly, either. At the moment, there wasn't anything that they could say. Trapped—prisoners where they could only be found by a miracle—witnessing with their own eyes a victory that they would have gladly have given their lives to prevent—they were both speechless with frustration.

"YOUR SILENCE is most gratifying!" came Zytoff's voice again. "It is a greater compliment than anything you could say in words. And now, there are many things to be done. I must arrange for your trip back, Lieutenant Brooks. The captain, I believe I will detain as my guest for a while longer. There are others who may wish to see him in person."

Dusty looked at Curly.

"Never mind me, kid," he said. "You know what you're to do. The hell with me! Get it? The hell with me!"

Zytoff cut in before Curly could say anything. He spoke as he shook his head.

"There is nothing that he could do for you, captain. Perhaps I did not make myself plain. When Lieutenant Brooks returns to his friends, he will remember nothing. It will be the same as awakening from a sound sleep."

"Nuts!" Dusty cut in harshly.

"Perhaps," was the quiet comment. "But when Lieutenant Brooks recovers from the effects of the sleep gas I shall administer to him, he will have no memory of what has taken place. In fact, it is doubtful if he will have any memory of anything in his life. It will be as though he were reborn and starting life anew."

"Wonderful!" Dusty snapped at him. "I suppose you thought it all up by yourself. You're just full of inventions, aren't you? What do you think this is, the year three thousand, or something?"

Zytoff smiled.

"I don't think, I know, captain," he said. "But we are wasting time. Say good-by to your friend, and then the guard will take you back to your rooms."

Dusty glanced at Curly. But Brooks was not looking at him. The lean pilot's eyes were riveted on a table near the wall. On the table were several charts and sheets of paper covered with figures and notations.

A quick look at them made Dusty's heart leap. Maybe he was wrong—but were those papers the original formula, with the additional findings of the Black chemist?

As the thought flashed to him, he saw Curly take a quick step forward and kick out with his right foot. It hit the edge of the table, tipped it up, and the papers on the top went sliding off—sliding off and down into the stone tray of molten metal.

The little gray-haired chemist screamed insanely and tried to dash forward. Instantly Dusty thrust out his foot, tripped the man and sent him flying.

Zytoff roared and slashed at Dusty with all his might. Though off balance the Yank was able to roll a bit with the blow. But not enough. He felt as though the base of his skull had been split wide open.

Through a red blaze he saw the Black guards pounding Curly Brooks down onto his knees. And he also saw the Black chemist striving to claw burning papers from out of the stone tray of molten metal. But even as the Black touched them they became charred powder in his hand.

And then the red haze deepened before his eyes—blotted out everything, and he knew that he was falling over backward, flat on the floor.

CHAPTER 11
HELL'S PASSAGEWAY

SHARP STINGING pains shooting through his face brought Dusty back to consciousness. Opening his eyes, he saw Curly bending over him. The lean pilot was methodically smacking him first on one cheek and then on the other with the flat of his hand. Dusty groaned, twisted to one side.

"Hey, easy!" he muttered. "I'm okay."

Curly stopped, helped Dusty up to a sitting position. Getting a grip on himself Dusty looked about. They were in an empty room that contained nothing but a single door. On the floor next to him were lengths of chewed rope. As he raised his eyes from the rope to Curly's face, his pal nodded.

"Broke every fingernail and most of my teeth," Brooks said. "But we're free until they come back, anyway."

Dusty was still in a haze.

129

"How'd we get here?" he grunted. "I thought you passed out, too."

"Almost, but not quite," replied Curly. "They were more excited about trying to save those papers. By God, I really think that we've put them back at scratch again. They must have been the formula!"

"Let's hope so!" Dusty muttered thickly. "And my hats off to you, Curly. Hell, I'd have never thought of that. But I can't understand why either of us is still alive!"

As he spoke he looked at the door. Curly followed his gaze.

"And it's not locked," he said with startling suddenness. "It's unlocked, and it leads out into some kind of a corridor. They lugged us back and tossed us in here. I was a bit groggy, but I think that we're on the same level as that assembly room. I don't recall their lugging us down any stairs."

Dusty started to get up, then sank back again with a puzzled frown.

"Wonder what the trick is?" he murmured softly. "No guards, and a door that's unlocked. That sounds just a wee bit screwy to me. Say, how long have we been here anyway?"

"About an hour, as near as I can judge," replied Brooks. Then, "Well—shall we stick around? What the hell do you think I woke you up for, Dusty?"

Dusty pushed himself up on his feet, leaned against the wall a couple of seconds, then moved toward the door.

"Okay," he said. "If it's a trick, we might as well find out what it's all about. Come on!"

Curly tagging his heels, he reached the door, opened it a foot or so, and stuck his head out. Nothing greeted him but an empty corridor. He hesitated a couple of seconds, then pulled the door open wide and stepped out into the corridor.

No crash of a gun, and no roar of a voice calling to him to halt. Silence, and a lot of it. Halfway along the right side of the corridor was another door. Shrugging, he moved toward it.

When he reached it, he stopped and stood listening intently. But he couldn't hear a single thing. He glanced at Curly. Brooks grimaced and arched his eyebrows.

"Try it," he whispered.

The door knob yielded to Dusty's touch. He twisted it and slowly pushed the door open. If he expected to see something unusual, he was very much disappointed. There was a room beyond the door—a room as completely empty as the one they had just left.

With a grunt he released his grip on the doorknob and continued on down the corridor to a door at the far end. Its knob did not yield to his touch, however. It didn't twist the fraction of an inch, and when he put the pressure of his shoulder against the door, he realized that it was heavily bolted on the other side. Straightening up, he gave Curly a twisted smile.

"That's that!" he said. "Didn't have to put a guard on us. We're locked up tight as a drum. But I still can't figure why we're still alive."

"Maybe, he thinks we're still valuable to him," Curly shrugged. "Though I'm damned if I can see it."

Dusty stood glaring at the bolted door.

"I can make a wild guess, now that I think it over," he said, as thought talking to himself. "If the bum wasn't kidding about being able to gas you so that you'd wake up without any memory—and I'm inclined to believe everything he says—he probably intends to carry on with the job. It would work out perfect for him."

"How come?" frowned Curly. "I don't follow you. Jack and Biff still know that I headed for the Montana Rockies."

"Quite true," said Dusty. "But look at it this way—supposing you were picked up wandering around a thousand miles from here? You couldn't remember what happened—to you or to the ship. Don't you see—it would look as thought you'd run into trouble a thousand miles from here. Dammed if I know just how to put it in words. I—"

"I guess I get you," Curly interrupted. "It would be cockeyed enough for Jack to forget the Rocky Mountain angle for awhile, eh?"

"Something like that," nodded Dusty. Then through tightly drawn lips, "But assuming it's all on the schedule, we've got to beat them to it—got to get out of here. I think that what you did in the laboratory has given us an added bit of time. It's knocked them out of stride, I guess."

"Yeah!" echoed Curly gloomily. "But what do we do, now? Hell, what can we do?"

Dusty didn't reply. The germ of a thought was flitting around at the back of his brain; a tiny thread of memory that he was striving desperately to recall. He knew instinctively that it should have a very definite bearing on their present situation and immediate plans for changing it. Closing his eyes tight, he concentrated on snaring the illusive thought germ.

And then, suddenly, out of a clear sky it came to him. He spun around, grabbed Curly's arm and started dragging him back down the corridor. At the half open door he stopped, looked inside with heart thumping against his ribs. A second later he heaved a long sigh of thankfulness, pulled Curly into the room and shut the door.

"Say," began Curly, "what—"

"Shut up!" Dusty clipped. "I think I've found the way out. When they nailed me with paralytic gas in that other room, the gas came in through the ventilator—one just like that one up there. Get it? There's just the hope that we can wiggle through it and get out."

Curly's eyes opened wide, and his body trembled as he looked at the ventilator opening high up on the opposite wall.

"Is—do you think it's big enough?" he asked, as though reluctant to speak the words.

"It's got to be!" said Dusty grimly. "Come on—no wait a second!"

Turning back toward the door, he slid home a bolt that was on the inside.

"We may be able to use the time it will take them to break it in," he said. "Now, up with you, kid. I'll pull myself up after you're in."

Curly shook his head.

"You'd never be able to make it," he said. "Nix—up you go, and I'll try to entertain them as long as I can when they come."

Dusty grabbed him, shoved him toward the wall.

"Don't be a fool!" he hissed. "Up with you, dammit! Don't worry, I'll make it!"

BEFORE CURLY had a chance to continue the argument, Dusty linked his fingers under Brooks' right foot and heaved upward. It was simple for Curly to cup his fingers over the lip of the ventilator and pull himself through. The moment he was entirely inside, Dusty backed over to the door, steadied himself a moment, then took three quick, springy steps and leaped up, hands flung upward and forward.

For a split second his body hung poised in mid-air, then it dropped. At that instant Dusty's fingers found the lip of the ventilator opening. His body crashed up against the wall, and he felt that his arms were being pulled from their sockets. But with eyes closed and teeth clenched he hung on for grim life.

When the pendulum movement of his body stopped, he sucked in his breath and pulled himself upward inch by inch. Finally he was able to crook his right forearm over the lips of the ventilator. Presently he had his left forearm up, and he was gasping for breath, head and shoulders inside the dark opening and the rest of him dangling into the room behind.

Something struck against his face. It was Curly's foot. Then he heard the soft whisper.

"Grab hold of it—I'll pull you the rest of the way."

Shifting his body he linked the fingers of one hand about Curly's ankle, and pushed out with the other for bracing support. Then began some of the toughest moments of his entire life.

Every muscle in his body seemed to be drawn as taut as a

piano wire, and every bone in his body seemed ready to snap in two at the very next second. But finally, though, the fact that he was stretched out flat on rough pine boards, and completely inside the ventilator opening pierced itself through his brain. Curly's anxious whisper was drifting back to him.

"Okay? Are you okay, kid? You let go of my foot!"

"Yeah, I guess so," Dusty heard himself whisper. "Can you see anything up ahead?"

During the moment or two of silence that followed, Dusty raised his head and tried to peer past Curly's body in front of him. But it was too dark to see anything. By feeling around he knew that they were in a two-by-three-foot boarded shaft. Somewhere far up ahead, the shaft came out of the mountain. At least he figured that such must be the case, for he could feel cold air blowing against his cheek. Then Curly's voice came softly back to him.

"Can't see a thing, yet. There's some sort of a light ahead, though. Okay?"

Dusty nodded in the darkness, rapped his knuckles against the sole of Curly's boot.

"Get going," he whispered. "But not too fast."

Unable to get all the way up on his hands and knees, Dusty raised himself up as much as the confined quarters would allow, and started crawling after Curly.

Progress was painfully slow, and when several moments later Dusty twisted his head and succeeded in looking back along the shaft, he calculated that they were not more than twenty yards from their starting point.

135

He did notice, however, that the shaft sloped gradually upward. That fact jacked up his hopes. Perhaps this shaft was separated from the others and led straight outside. He hoped like hell that it did.

Regardless of the fact that their predicament would be little changed—they'd be marooned far up the side of a snow-covered mountain, with God knew how many miles between them and help—it would be something just to be in the open air again. Maybe they'd even see the sun. There must be a sun shining somewhere.

Scraps of crazy, disjoined thoughts rambling through his head, he continued to crawl forward a few inches at a time. Repeatedly he ran his face up against one of Curly's feet. In the heavy, almost stifling darkness it was practically impossible to maintain a pace steady with that of Curly up ahead.

Presently, without warning, he rammed his head up against something that wasn't shoe leather. It was hard, and immovable, and contact with it made stars whirl before his eyes.

Choking back the curse that came to his lips he felt ahead with one hand, and touched a solid vertical beam. He felt nothing to the right of it, nor to the left.

"Curly!" he hissed. "Where are you?"

"Right here!" came the answer. "What's the trouble?"

Dusty placed his pal's voice to the left, and ahead. Instantly he realized what it was all about. They had reached a point in the shaft where another shaft joined it, or else it joined the other.

Curly had continued on to the left, but he had banged his

head up against the intersection post. He heard Curly wiggling back toward him. He reached out and stopped his pal's feet when they were but inches from his face.

"What's wrong, Dusty?"

"The shaft forks here, did you know that?"

There was the sharp intake of breath from Curly.

"Hell no! Must have missed it completely. Which one do you want to take? I can still see a bit of light way up ahead in this one. I think it curves to the left."

"Okay then," Dusty whispered. "Go on—"

He bit down hard on the rest, grabbed Curly's foot as a signal not to move. At that moment from somewhere far down the right-hand shaft came a weird sound.

It was so faint that he wondered for a second if his ears were playing him tricks. The sound was something like a shrill scream coming from far, far away. Not a continuous sound though. It appeared to break itself off repeatedly—short, jerky, yet always the same note.

"You hear that, Curly?"

"Hear what? I can't hear a damn thing?"

"Then shut up!" hissed Dusty. "Let me listen some more."

RELAXING HIS body, he tried to peer ahead in the pitch-dark shaft, and strained his ears to pick up the eerie sound again. For a full minute he didn't hear a thing save the thumping of his own heart. And then, he did—heard it plainly and distinctly—and this time the sound of it sent the blood surging through his reins.

"Curly!" he whispered excitedly. "We go along this shaft to the right. I'm going in now. Back up and follow me!"

Shoring to the side with his hands, Dusty pushed his body into the right shaft. When he was completely in it, he stopped and twisted his head so that his whispered words could carry down past his body.

"You set, kid?"

A hand grabbed his ankle and squeezed.

"Okay! But, why this way? What's up?"

"Listen!" Dusty hissed. "Can you hear it now?"

He pressed himself against the side, as though in doing so he'd make it possible for the faint sound up ahead to get past his body to Curly's ears. A couple of moments later, came Curly's startled gasp. "God! Unless I'm hearing things, that's a high-speed wireless set in action!"

"You're dead right!" Dusty whispered back. "And that gives me a whole lot of swell ideas. Come on—we're going to town!"

CHAPTER 12
S.O.S. EMERGENCY!

WITHOUT WAITING for Curly to make further comment, Dusty started crawling forward again as quickly and as silently as he could. Though it was pitch dark he realized that the shaft swung to the right and downward. There it leveled off and seemed to slope upward again.

Every so often he stopped, checked the sound, which was

getting louder and louder, and waited for Curly to bump into his feet before moving on again.

Once when he stopped, he didn't hear the sound. And for a moment his heart stood still for fear that he'd done what Curly did—gone right on past an intersection and not realized it. But when he heard it once more—now a clear high-keyed whine—he let out a grunt of marked relief and continued on.

Bump!

In the darkness he had blindly kept right on going until he had hit the wall of the turn with his head. Twisting to the right, he glanced ahead and promptly forgot the lingering pain in his head.

About twenty yards from him the shaft was cut by an oblong of yellow light. In other words, there was a ventilator opening connecting it with some room. And from that room, up through the ventilator and along the shaft, came the jerky whine of a high speed wireless set.

Twenty yards—sixty feet—and then what?

Inch by inch he wormed his way forward the last few feet, and then flattening out on his stomach, he peered cautiously around the edge of the ventilator opening. He found himself looking into a complete radio and wireless signal station.

To his right, diligently bent over a high-speed key, was a figure in the uniform of a Black Invader. Over his head was a set of receiving phones, and as he tapped the key with one hand, he adjusted instruments in front of him with the other.

To the Black's left, and almost opposite Dusty's position, was a door to the room, It was open a couple of inches, and as Dusty squinted past the opening his heart looped over. Beyond was the big domed airplane assembly room!

Because of the small opening and the angle at which he was looking into the domed room, he was unable to see whether the movable front was opened or not. At the moment, though, he didn't much care. The object of immediate importance was the Black crouched over the wireless key.

Holding his breath, Dusty stuck his head out into the room and glanced quickly straight downward. About two feet down the wall was a voltage meter. At least, in the split second he allowed himself, that's what he judged it to be.

He was content that it was at least something solid upon which he could brace a foot when he flung himself the six short feet of air space that separated him from the Black.

Pulling his head back into the shaft, he twisted as much as he could and groped back with one of his hands, at the same time jack-knifing his knees. Curly's hand resting on one of his feet came up with it. He grabbed the hand, and using a tight squeeze for a dash and a short light squeeze for a dot, he signaled d-o-n-t m-o-v-e in International Morse. As he stopped Curly squeezed o-k-e in reply.

Freeing his hand, Dusty twisted silently over on his side, caught hold of the near edge of the ventilator opening with both his hands, and pulled himself forward until his head and shoulders were out into the room.

Every instant of the time he kept his eyes glued on the figure at the key—and every split second of the time he breathed a

DUSTY CAME PILING DOWN ON THE BLACK

fierce prayer that the Black's ear-phones would shut off any outside sounds.

Holding himself from spilling into the room by his right hand, he doubled his body, drew his left leg up under him, and got it out into the room. He was now in the position of a high jumper going over the bar in what is known as the Western Roll. Further twisting his body made it possible for him to get his left foot down on the top of the voltage meter.

But as he did that, the Black stopped tapping the key, pulled the phones from his ears and started to turn around. Jet-black eyes, heavy from want of sleep, met Dusty's.

For an instant they blinked in half stupid amazement, then went wide with wild alarm. What they did after that, Dusty didn't know. His body was catapulting through space, and his eyes were riveted on the fang-toothed mouth that was opening to let out a mighty roar. It did let out the first part of it, and then a frenzied American came piling down on its owner with the force of a catapulted ton of bricks.

As he plowed down on the man, Dusty shoved upward and forward with his hands. He felt leathery skin between his clawing fingers, locked them in it and squeezed with every ounce of his strength.

The momentum of the drop, however, was too great for him to maintain his hold. His hands were torn lose, and the arm of the Black's chair smashed against his shoulder and twisted him over on his side. For a couple of seconds his whole arm from wrist to shoulder socket went completely numb.

Squirming underneath him, half jammed against the floor

and the radio table, the Black suddenly gave a hoarse, choking grunt and heaved up like a cat arching its back. Through a filming haze Dusty saw a rage-twisted face glaring up at him, saw a hammerhead fist, rushing for his head.

In that infinitesimal period of time that his brain took to register that fact, he knew that he would not be able to avoid that plunging fist—knew that it was going to catch him square on the jaw with the force of the Chicago-New York streamlined express.

And then, something very queer happened. The plowing fist stopped short in mid-air, dropped down out of sight. And the rage-twisted face took on a dull and vacant expression.

The eyes actually fluttered closed and the jaw sagged open. And it was just about a couple of seconds after that, Dusty realized the fact that Curly Brooks was pulling him up on his feet. The knuckles of Curly's right fist were bleeding. There were blood marks on the limp Black's jaw.

Swaying as he tried to steady himself against the wireless table, Dusty gaped foolishly at his pal. Once again Curly had played Johnny-on-the-spot and saved him from a lot of trouble. Right now, Curly was occupied with shutting the door; and sliding a bolt into place. He came right back, lips twisted in a half grin.

"Swell idea!" he whispered. "But your execution was just a bit lousy. Glad I was along."

By now Dusty was fully recovered from his wild plunge down onto the floor.

"Yeah!" he nodded vigorously. "So'm I. Thanks. I'll do the same for you sometime."

As he talked, he swept his eyes about the room, spotted the radio transmitter on the far side. Turning back to Curly, he pointed at the Black stretched out on the floor.

"Take his gun, and watch him!" he said. "This is what we're here for. I'm going to send out an S.O.S. Emergency. No matter what may happen to us, we've got to let the others know."

Curly nodded grimly, didn't speak. It was no time for that kind of talk now. He simply bent over and took the holstered gun away from the unconscious Black.

Then, after a split second's mental debate, he reversed the gun in his hand and slammed the butt down on the Black's right temple. Then he went over and took up a position by the door.

IN THE meantime, Dusty had leaped across the room to the radio transmitter, and was feverishly snapping on contact switches and spinning the wave-length and volume dials. Then with fingers that trembled he scooped up the transmitter tube from out of its cradle. "S.O.S. Emergency—all American stations!" he barked into it. "This is a general alarm from Captain Ayres. Black Invaders have established a secret assembly airdrome near M-Twenty Six in the Rocky Mountains. Send planes and troop transports to capture and destroy it at once. Personal to Agent 10 or X-Thirty-four at Washington H.Q. Enemy has discovered secret of Metal-Meltic. Exert every effort to destroy their hiding place near M-Twenty Six. Look for snow-packed shelf with trees. S.O.S. Emergency! For God's sake send all help possible.

144

We've captured the radio-room, but I don't know how long we can—"

There was an exploding sound in the set, and the green signal light to the left of the panel winked out. At the same time every one of the recording dial needles dropped back to the zero peg.

One sweeping glance and Dusty knew that the set had been put out of commission from the outside—undoubtedly from an adjoining power-room.

He dropped the transmitter tube back into the cradle, and turned around toward Curly.

"Cut off before a check-back could come through," he grunted. "All we can do now is hope. I guess they're wise to what's happened."

Brooks shrugged, fingered the gun he held in his hand.

"We could make a run for it," he said with a side nod toward the door. "I'll go first and use this—maybe you'll be able to get through. Even if one of us—"

He stopped as Dusty shook his head.

"No?"

"No!"

"Well, think up a better idea then! It's a cinch we can't just sit here."

"Why not?" Dusty broke in quietly. "They're—by God, holding everything!"

With a startling suddenness that caused Curly Brooks to scowl at him darkly, Dusty bounded across the room, and dropped down on his hands and knees by a big four-foot box under a table in the corner. The heavy lid to the box was not locked, and with a grunt he flung it up open. Looking inside, he let out a whoop of joy.

"Are they good to us!" he exclaimed. "Look, Curly—see what Santa has left for us!"

Curly bounded over, and stared down into the box. Its contents consisted of half a dozen sub-machine guns practically all assembled and ready for use. Only the stocks needed to be locked into place. And as Dusty dived in with both hands and unsnapped one of the cartridge drums, they both saw that it was completely loaded—loaded with wicked looking slugs!

"Well, I'll be—"

Curly's exclamation died on his lips. From beyond the door a machine gun snarled into life, and hissing steel came slicing through the wood as though it were so much cheese. Dusty felt something tug at his left sleeve as he dropped flat and pulled Curly down on top of him.

"Roll, kid!" he snapped. "Roll to the left!"

His sharp order was unnecessary. Curly was already rolling over and over and out of line with the door. Dusty followed him, then flattened out and reached back for the machine-gun case.

As more steel slugs cut through the wood of the door and finished up in instruments and meters fitted to the back wall, he pulled the case close, reached in and took out the parts of two guns. A stock and a barrel he gave to Curly, who accepted it without a word and promptly put it together. A stock and a barrel he kept for himself, and did the same thing.

"Now!" he grated softly, swinging the muzzle of the gun

around to bear on the splintered and cracked door, "let 'em try to come and get us!"

As though his words were a sort of signal to those outside, the firing stopped, and the voice of Zytoff came through to them.

"You have sealed your doom, you two dogs!" he roared. "You will never leave there alive!"

"That's okay with us, just as long as you join the party!" Dusty shouted back. "I told you, Zytoff, that you were riding for a surprise! And it'll be here, right soon!"

A load booming laugh greeted his words.

"You poor fool? Do you think for an instant that your message got through to anyone?"

Dusty winked at Curly's tight-lipped expression.

"Of course not!" he called back. "You only put the set out of commission just to see if you could, didn't you? Why you poor boob, think up another one!"

THAT REMARK was greeted by another savage burst of machine-gun fire, and the instrument-covered wall some ten or twelve feet from where the two Yanks crouched became splintered and shattered shambles. Out the corner of his eye, Dusty saw Curly level his gun, start to crook his finger on the trigger. He reached out and knocked the gun down.

"Nix, kid, nix!" he hissed. "What they don't know is duck soup for us! They may try to rush us—then that'll be our time to let drive. We've got to stall for time—got to let them wonder whether we're armed or not. Don't let on until we have to!"

Curly relaxed his grip on the gun and his eyes unconsciously wandered up toward the ventilator opening. Dusty saw the look that came into them, and knew instantly what Brooks was thinking about—would the Blacks try to gas them through the ventilator opening?

Dusty doubted it—doubted it very much. The shaft was empty, and it would take a lot of precious time to lead a hose through; have one of them crawl through with it.

The shaft in that other room, the room where he had been gassed, must have been shorter, or at least considerably more accessible than this one. Nope! It was a million to one that Zytoff would not try to gas them.

"Not a chance," he spoke his thoughts aloud to Curly. "They don't dare take the time. Besides, they know I'd be wise to them this time. And another thing, the draft is toward that door they've been smacking—they'd get a few whiffs out there."

"Captain Ayres!"

The voice of Zytoff came through the door.

"Captain Ayres! I'm willing to bargain with you. Come out of there, both of you, and I promise to spare your lives. Remain, and you will die!"

The two Yanks looked at each other, each with a puzzled glint in his eyes. Their thoughts at the moment were the same. How come Zytoff was getting big hearted? How come he was willing to permit them to live? It was Dusty who spoke that thought aloud.

"What's the big idea, Zytoff?" he shouted. "Why not come in and get us? That'll be more fun for you!"

"Your answer!" thundered the Black. "Do you wish to save

your lives and come out—my sacred promise on that—or do you wish to remain and die? My most sacred promise on that, too. Speak up—which shall it be?"

Dusty didn't answer directly. A heavy scowl on his face, he tried to figure Zytoff's reason for wanting them to leave the room. Rather, why was he so keen about it, that he was willing to spare their lives?

The Black knew that their call for help had gone out over the air. His bluff remark to them had fallen flat. Therefore he must know that American planes were right now churning air toward the spot. Did he think that the place was so well hidden that the relief pilots would not spot it? Or—

"Got it!" he suddenly exclaimed. "Hell yes, of course!"

"Got what?" Curly snapped at him.

Dusty leaned close to him, hardly spoke above a whisper.

"The radio is on the blink, but the wireless is still okay! That's what he wants to get in for. Wants to send out for a bit of help himself. Don't you see—they haven't got enough of their planes assembled yet and he doesn't dare pull out with what he has got. The wireless set—that's what he wants! Quick—slide over to that opposite corner!"

As he spoke the last he gave Curly a shove. The lean pilot scuttled across the floor to the corner indicated. Dusty followed at his heels, twisted around and raised his submachine gun.

"Hey, Zytoff!" he shouted, cupping one hand to his lips so as to offset the direction of his voice. "Hey, you out there!"

"Your answer!" came back the thundering words. "I will count five!"

"Save your breath, sweetheart!" Dusty hurled back at him. "The wireless set is a swell target—lots of glass to break! Listen!"

Dusty squeezed the trigger of the sub-machine gun and swung the gun back and forth. Flame and clattering sound spurted from the muzzle and the wireless instruments on the side wall jumped and jerked, splintered and shattered, and went spilling down onto the floor in small pieces.

"That's our answer!" Dusty roared as he ceased firing. "And my original tip still goes—pack up and drift, you bum!"

CHAPTER 13
THE CYCLONE ACE

UTTER SILENCE greeted Dusty's taunting remark. Though both Yanks strained their ears they heard not a single sound from beyond the bullet-shattered door.

For three full minutes everything remained as still as death, and then suddenly there came to them a familiar noise that jerked them both up straight. It was the noise of an airplane engine roaring into life. Like a streak of light Dusty was up on his feet.

"We were right, kid!" he yelled. "It was the wireless set. Now they're taking French leave!"

"Or maybe to signal from the air!" Curly put in. "Hey, don't be a dope—some of them may still be waiting out there!"

Dusty stopped short, hugged close to the near wall.

"Maybe you're right," he said under his breath. "But the job isn't done yet—we even can't let him get away. We've got to hold them here, bottled up, until the others arrive. Here, give me a hand!"

With quick movements Dusty darted across the room, grabbed hold of the unconscious radio operator and dragged the limp figure over next to the door. Hooking his gun arm around the man he reached out his other hand and slid back the bolt. Then he twisted back to Curly.

"This egg goes first!" he whispered. "He draws the fire, then we dive through. The front of that room must be to the left. And it's open, or we wouldn't have heard that plane. Let drive at anything you see. Okay?"

Curly tightened his lips.

"Okay, kid!"

Twisting back, Dusty shifted his arm holding the Black. Then pushing the splintered door, he wedged his toe in the crack, and swayed back against the wall. A quick shoving kick of his foot and the door slammed open.

In the same split second he hurled the form of the radio operator through the opening. Instantly, clatter of machine-gun and rifle fire broke out.

Crouched low behind the Black, Dusty sensed the man's body twisting and jerking. But he himself was already in motion—diving head first through the doorway, sub-machine gun flung out in front of him.

One flash glance of a domed room and of walls lined with semi-assembled airplane parts, then he saw a group of figures crouched down on the floor to his left. In one movement he swung the gun and squeezed the trigger. At practically the same instant he crashed down onto the floor. But he hardly felt the pains that went shooting through his body. He was only conscious of the crouching group scurrying for cover—of their flinging up their hands and sprawling down to lay still as the steel slugs from his chattering gun slashed and tore into them.

A moment later, though, he was conscious of another gun banging out sound practically inside his head. He half twisted and saw Curly's gun not six inches from his head slapping out sound and flame straight ahead. As he twisted back he saw an iron-gray-haired little man spin around like a top and drop flat. Three other Blacks in back of him went down like ten-pins.

So fast had the action been that everything was but a flashing general picture—no time for minute details. But as Dusty twisted over to take up a position behind an engine crate, he suddenly cut short his movement and plunged to his knees with a roaring curse.

The front side of the domed room was opened, as he had guessed. And right now an all-red monoplane with prop ticking over, was taxiing swiftly toward the opening past the sheltering trees on the right side. Through the opening he could see some Dart pursuits swinging around on the snow packed shelf to take off.

Those two facts, however, were not the cause of his roaring curse. On the contrary, it was sight of a figure running toward another plane. Running toward his plane, the Silver Flash!

Totally oblivious to stray bullets that crackled and whined past his ears, Dusty lunged to his feet and started racing madly across the wood floor of the domed room.

"Like hell you will! Like hell you will!"

He drowned out his own words when he squeezed the trigger of his gun. The Black tearing toward the Flash—Dusty realized that it wasn't Zytoff—started dodging this way and that, zigzagging in a frantic attempt to keep clear of Dusty's hissing hail of steel.

That he, himself, was being shot at, Dusty didn't even realize, so intent was he upon the Black thirty yards away.

He didn't even feel the invisible fingers that plucked at the loose folds of his flying suit. He simply kept the trigger squeezed and tried desperately to bring the gun to bear on the darting, twisting figure ahead.

It was the Black's own fault. At least it seemed to appear that way. With only ten yards or so to go to reach the shelter of the Flash's cockpit, the Black stopped zigzagging and made a final lunging sprint straight forward.

He covered five of those ten yards, and then the slugs from Dusty's gun caught him square in the back. The force of their impact carried the Black the remaining five yards, but he was stone dead, a couple of pounds of hot steel in his body, when he crashed up against the fuselage of the Flash and rebounded onto the floor.

Unable to check his own speed, Dusty continued to pound forward, still firing. And then Fate took a crack at him. Something slapped against the barrel of his gun, wrenching it from his clawing fingers and sending it spinning off into space.

In an effort to hang onto the gun, he unconsciously threw himself off balance. Too late he tried to correct the mistake.

His right foot caught behind his left knee, refused to go forward. As though he had run straight smack into a taut wire, his legs stopped dead and the rest of him went arcing over and down. Somehow he managed to drop his hands and break the fall a bit as he hit the floor. But momentum was still having a holiday, and in a perfect belly-slide he skidded into the dead body of the Black and carried it right along as he went sliding clear under the fuselage of the Flash.

GROGGY AND almost completely winded, he nevertheless pulled himself up onto his feet. He heard a machine gun crash to his left, turned that way just in time to see a Black mechanic do a neat backward loop down onto the floor, and Curly Brooks come tearing around the tail of the Silver Flash.

Dusty gaped down at his own bleeding hands and realizing that they longer held a gun, bent over to grab the dead Black's holstered automatic. Curly, however, grabbed him, and pulled him back.

"Never mind!" he shouted. "I can hold these bums—only a couple left in the room. Into the Flash—get that all-red crate! Get it! Warn the others about what it can do. Get going in the Flash!"

Dusty scowled, shook his head. He couldn't leave Curly down here.

But Curly's mind was made up. He caught hold of Dusty with both hands, practically lifted him up onto the fuselage step.

"It's up to you, Dusty!" he roared. "Warn them—warn the

others! They've arrived—you can hear them up there! For God's sake, get going! I'll be okay!"

The air was now vibrating from the roar of airplane engines high up in the winter sky, and as Dusty forked into the cockpit and lunged his foot down on the electric starter he knew that not all of them were Black Invader engines. In other words, Curly was right—Yank planes answering his frantic radio S.O.S. Emergency, had arrived. But up there waiting for them, was Zytoff and his remaining supply of Metal-Meltic.

A hesitant glance back at Curly just long enough to see the lean pilot shake his head vigorously and go darting behind a protecting row of half mounted engines, and then Dusty released the wheel brakes and kicking rudder, sent the Flash swinging around and taxiing swiftly toward the opening on the right.

As he shot out into the open, onto a glistening shelf of hard packed snow, he dully realized everything was tinged with the crimson rays of a sinking sun—realized that it must be well past mid-afternoon. When had he last seen the sun? Must have been a couple of thousand years ago wasn't it?

The crazy question went unanswered. At that moment he was staring up into the sky past towering snow-covered mountain peaks—staring up at a skyful of twisting, turning planes. Most of them were American. But high above the whirling pack was a red monoplane, swinging about in slow ever-widening circles. It gave Dusty the flash impression of being a great red vulture waiting for the exact moment to swoop down on its victims.

Keeping his eyes glued to it, he slammed open the throttle,

sent the Flash racing across the hard snow, and pulled it clear. Holding the nose up a maximum climbing angle he started to shoot out his free hand toward the radio panel, when at that moment he saw the red light blinking. He continued the movement however, snapped on contact and twisted the wave-length dial knob to S.O.S. Emergency reading.

"All Yank—"

The ear-phones' crackling sound, checked him. Startling words banged against his ear-drums.

"All Yank planes! This is Ayres—Captain Ayres! I've captured the red ship above you! Spread out for formation. I'm coming down to join you! Yank planes—attention! I'm coming down to join you in the red plane; spread out into formation!"

For a second Dusty couldn't think. He'd heard his own booming voice in his own ear-phones! Own voice? Own voice, hell! It was Zytoff! Damn his rotten hide. He was trying to draw the Yanks out for a wholesale slaughter—trap them all at once with his blasted Metal-Meltic.

In one continuous lightning-like movement Dusty spun on full transmission volume and grabbed up the transmitter tube.

"Yanks! Yanks!" he howled. "It's a damn lie—look out, look out for the red crate! This is Dusty, in the Flash—in the Silver Flash below you. For God's sake keep clear of that red plane. Don't let it come down to you—keep under it!"

Dusty groaned, pulled the nose up so that the Flash was almost at the vertical. The twenty-eight hundred horses cowled into the nose roared and bellowed in protest. But Dusty didn't even notice it as he watched the red monoplane come rushing down in a long slanting dive toward a group of Yank planes directly below it.

"Look out—don't let that ship get close to you! Look out for the red plane!"

Even as Dusty shouted his second warning, he knew that it was falling on deaf ears. The Yanks directly under Zytoff's diving ship were making no effort to get out of its way. Perhaps they were deaf, or perhaps they hadn't troubled to tune in on his warning. But at any rate, they were fast approaching their doom.

When the red plane was but a couple of hundred feet above them, it suddenly spun around on wing, streaked back a short distance, then in a curving dive came sweeping back under them. At that instant, pale blue smoke streamed out from the two flanged pipe ends mounted on the rudder post. The flat, wavy ribbons of blue merged together, darkened in hue, and spread out in an ever widening V-shaped layer.

TOO LATE the American pilots saw the danger. Three of the planes dived down through the wavy blue. Instantly they ceased to be airplanes, and became huge drops of flaming molten metal plunging earthward.

The blue cyclone that cut its flat path across the heavens was as a wavy gateway to utter oblivion. Shouting at the top of his voice, Dusty saw two, three, and four American planes plunge down into it—actually saw their metal snouts become drops of fire, while the rear section of the plane, still above the blue hell, was as yet untouched. A fifth American pilot tried frantically in the last remaining second to pull up and away. But his diving speed was too great, and his left wings swept through the stuff as he tried to arc up. Metal spars, ribs, and wing covering became molten fire. The unbalanced plane flopped over on its other side and the whole thing dropped down into the blue cyclone of death.

As the red plane cut around in a spinning turn in an effort to trap two other American ships, Dusty kicked rudder with all his might, and jabbed both trigger trips forward.

He knew instinctively that the range was too great. The Flash's engine had done its best. The plane was practically hovering motionless on its prop. Nothing—nothing could stop that pilot of the red plane now. The two Yank planes Zytoff was diving for would be caught cold.

And as Dusty snapped his eyes toward them, his heart seemed to turn to stone.

One of them, the nearest one, was an X-Diesel. On its fuselage were the personal markings of Biff Bolton!

Zytoff was almost on top of the two American planes—almost on the point of cutting back under them and thus trapping them between a double layer of his deadly blue hell when Dusty saw Biff Bolton's plane whip over and start down in a spin.

The pilot of the other craft was staking his all in an effort to skid sidewise out into the clear. He was partially succeeding, leaving Biff Bolton the lone target for Zytoff.

"Biff! Biff! For God's sake, move!" Dusty uttered the words in the same breath that he cursed the Flash on to greater speed. His Brownings were hammering out their messengers of death, but he was still too far away from the red plane. A moment later he was forced to cease fire altogether. A spinning twist of

Biff's plane brought it right into line with Dusty's fire. It wasn't Biff's fault, however. Had he not spun away at that exact moment his right wing would have swept through the blue layer.

The big pilot was still in danger, though. Whether Zytoff realized that his prey was Dusty's friend, or whether it was sheer savage determination to get another victim while his supply of Metal-Meltic held out—there was no telling. But at any rate, the Black was ignoring every other craft in the heavens, and concentrating on Biff. And Biff was flying a losing battle. Like the tentacles of some weird and horrible blue octopus, the wavy strands of Metal-Meltic were slowly but surely hemming In Biff's ship.

Dusty knew that it was but a matter of seconds. Unless something could be done to alter the present course of Zytoff's plane, good old Biff Bolton was doomed to a hellish death.

Reckless fury surged up in Dusty. He ceased to be a human being at the controls of a fleet sky chariot and he became a roaring, raving automatic machine of death. Without even giving the idea a single thought, he slammed the Flash around in wing-groaning turn and plunged it straight between two floating layers of blue death. Not a dozen feet separated either his upper or lower wings from the terrible stuff.

Hunched forward over the stick he felt as though he were streaking straight through the very bowels of hell itself. Feet, legs, hands, body and head seemed seared to a crisp. The world all about him was on fire.

And then he came streaking out from between the two layers. Streaking out, and heading straight for the red plane that was curving away from him—curving away to spew back over him its hissing oblivion.

"Not this time—or any other time, by God!"

The rasping sound of Dusty's shout blended in with the savage yammer of his two Brownings. At the same instant he hurled the Silver Flash to the left, darted clear of the trailing blue death, and cut back in again with the speed of a striking cobra. A wild yell of mad triumph spilled off his lips as he saw his slugs smash into Zytoff's ship. He knew that they were bouncing off armor plating, but right at the moment that didn't matter. They were coming too close to the glass cockpit cowl for comfort, and Zytoff was being driven away from Biff Bolton.

Foot by foot, yard by yard, the red ship swung away, leaving a great gaping hole of clear air through its twisted and interwoven blue web.

"Biff!" Dusty shouted. "Go down through that hole! Signal the other planes! Go down onto that shelf! Curly's there—he needs help! Go down to Curly. I'll take care of this mug!"

The red signal light blinked, and he heard Biff's thankful voice.

"Sure, skipper, sure! Gee, thanks! I'll go down! But I guess there isn't—"

The ear-phones made a clicking sound and went silent Dusty didn't waste the time or breath with a check-back. Biff had heard him and was going down to help Curly. Please God that Curly was still all right!

The thought of his pal down there alone; of Curly's sacrifice that he might go after Zytoff, sent Dusty's determination soaring up to the peak.

He banged his already wide open throttle with his fist, and cursed at the Flash as though it were actually something human, with ears. And every instant of the time he kept trying to edge in closer to the red plane—edge in close enough to let drive a fatal burst of shots. But there was no greenhorn pilot at the controls of that red ship. In fact, very far from it. Each passing second brought home that truth more forcibly to Dusty.

TRUE, ZYTOFF had the advantage. Streaming out from the top of his rudder post was a form of death far, far more effective than aerial machine-gun bursts. It not only covered a wider area, but it also prevented an attacker from getting into a cold-meat position.

But, apart from that, Zytoff was tossing his craft this way and that with every bit as much skill as any other pilot in the air. And at the same time that he kept clear of Dusty's bursts, he also made sure that he didn't back-track into the hell he was trailing across the sky.

With grim doggedness Dusty clung to him, however, followed through with every trick he did and slammed home a burst every time he got a chance. And then suddenly he realized what Zytoff was really trying to do.

Fully aware that the clinging Yank was too clever to be trapped by the Metal-Meltic, Zytoff was trying to make his escape—make his escape in a huge billowy cloud bank to the north.

Even as the truth came to him, Dusty heard the rapid jabbering of Black Invader jargon in his ear-phones. For no reason at all he threw back his head and looked up. There, a thousand feet above him were three Black Darts. They were tagging along at his speed but making no attempt to come down for fear, undoubtedly, of getting into Zytoff's trail of Metal-Meltic.

At least, that is the way it appeared to Dusty at that second. But as he snapped his eyes back to Zytoff's ship again, he saw something that brought a roar of surprise to his lips.

The blue hell was no longer coming out from the flanged pipe ends in a steady stream. It was jerky; popping out in short

DUSTY FOLLOWED HIM OVER

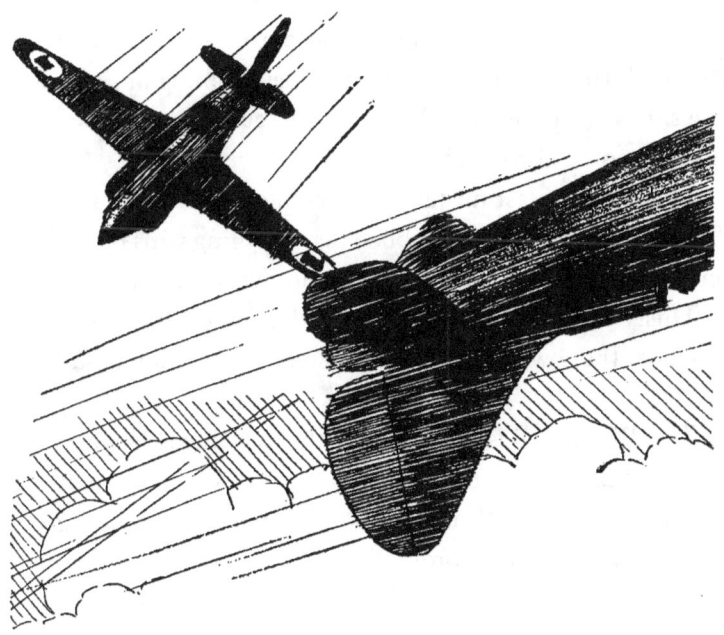

puffs that were practically whipped into oblivion by the prop wash. A second or two later the right pipe stopped gushing forth blue vapor altogether. And then the left pipe followed suit.

The reason was instantly obvious to Dusty. So was the crazy Black Invader jargon he had heard a few moments before. Zytoff's supply of Metal-Meltic had run out. His tanks were empty, and he had signaled to three of his pilots to cover his retreat.

As Dusty started to close in behind the red craft, slam in for a cold-meat burst, the fury of hell smacked down on him from above.

With that he rolled. A three-quarter roll, and then down he dropped. The left hand ship of the three zooming up, jerked to the side as its pilot tried desperately to cut off and curve back up for a sort of broadside attack.

That was the last mistake that its pilot made in this world. Dusty followed him over, jabbed his Browning trips home. The smoking steel slugs from the two muzzles did the rest.

Dusty didn't have time to watch the rest of the dead man's descent. There were still two of his gang in the air. And how, too!

Two Blacks against one Yank! In the next three seconds those Blacks must have thought it was the two of them against a couple of hundred Yanks. Feet and hands, and shooting eye working in perfect co-ordination, Dusty raced and spun and tore around them as though they were tied to a post.

One of them decided that he'd had too much, and in a vicious maneuver he spun down, leaving his pal to carry on with the good work. It was a yellow trick, but it did manage to save the Black's life.

His pal lived just about long enough to get a two-second look at the Silver Flash boring in. And then it was curtains! Armor plate or no armor plate, Dusty's savage fire practically blew the Dart apart in mid-air, and the Black went slithering earthward in small pieces.

"Now, that other tramp!"

But as Dusty hastily scanned the surrounding skies he relaxed his tensed muscles, and grunted. The other Dart was fading into the clouds a good four miles away, traveling at a speed that should put him over the North Pole in nothing flat. And as for Zytoff and his red plane—it was absolutely nowhere to be seen. It had long since faded out of sight.

Hardly realizing what a crazy quirk of his brain was causing him to do, Dusty grabbed up the transmitter tube, spun on full long-wave volume.

"Captain Ayres calling Zytoff!" he yelled. "Captain Ayres calling Zytoff. Drop in again, you bum, sometime when you can stay longer!"

He grinned at his spontaneous action, started to put the transmitter tube back on its hook, when the red light blinked and a pleasant voice spoke in the earphones.

"I will, captain, I promise you! And thank you for the invitation!"

AS THE red light blinked out, and the ear-phones went silent, Dusty snapped his eyes toward the station direction finder. As he noted the position of the recording needle, a split second before it dropped back to the "No Register" peg, he grinned tightly. Zytoff had been making tracks too. According to the station direction finder dial he had broadcast from about three hundred miles due north.

"I'll be waiting to greet you!" grunted Dusty and snapped off his own set.

But as he did, he suddenly let out a sharp curse, and spun the ship around on wing-tip and sent it roaring south over the snow-covered peaks. Curly! How was Curly making out? Had Biff and the others gone down to help him?

A group of towering peaks hid the shelf that formed the

secret drome. But as Dusty strained his eyes about the heavens through which he raced, he saw not the sign of a single plane, either Yank or Black Invader.

For several minutes he roared southward and a moment later he went roaring down over the edge of the circle of mountain peaks and saw the snow-packed ledge. It was not only snow-packed, but plane-packed as well. There seemed to be every damn ship in the U.S. air force squatted down there.

Cutting his throttle, Dusty curved down lower, picked out a narrow strip on the far side and headed toward it. Out the corner of his eye he saw figures running between the planes. But he didn't have time to take a good look at them. Landing on what space the others had left was not fledgling's undertaking.

Feet steady on the rudder pedals, hands firmly gripping the stick, he guided the Flash down the last few feet and allowed it to settle. He leaped out and started running toward the mountain side of the ledge.

"That you, Ayres?" A voice called to him but it wasn't one that he recognized, so he didn't stop.

"Hey, Ayres! What happened to you? We thought that you'd gone down."

Another voice that he didn't know and again he went on. Side-stepping parked plane wings, but not once checking his speed, he tore across the ledge, around the fringe of trees and through the opening on the right. Only then did he make any attempt to come to a halt.

The first thing he recognized was Biff Bolton's broad back. He fairly leaped at the big pilot, spun him around.

"Biff! Where's Curly? Is Curly all right? Speak up, damn you!"

"Sure I am—now! But they were just trying to tell me that you'd got yourself shot down!"

Dusty shoved Biff to one side and saw Curly, Jack Horner, Major Drake, and a few other pilots in a group. He leaped, grabbed hold of his pal and pounded him on the back.

"So it's you—are you okay?"

"Okay?" echoed Brooks. "Hell yes, I didn't have anything to do after you left. They scuttled for cover. And then some of the boys landed and gave me a hand. Transports with sappers to smoke out the place will be here soon. But Zytoff! Did he—"

Curly stopped.

"He did," nodded Dusty grimly. "But he took only memories with him—nothing else!" As Dusty spoke the last he looked at Agent 10. The Intelligence man knew what he meant and a grateful look came into his eyes. He took a step toward Dusty.

"I don't know what to say," he began in a choked voice. "I don't know how to thank—"

"Hell, thank him!" Dusty said, twisting him toward Curly. "He's the bright-haired boy of this show! All I did was to fall down so that he could be there to pick me up!"

"Nix on that!" Curly came back. "Skip it! One hero in Group Seven is enough! No need of giving the major two headaches!"

For once Dusty had no ready comeback. But he didn't care—just this once.

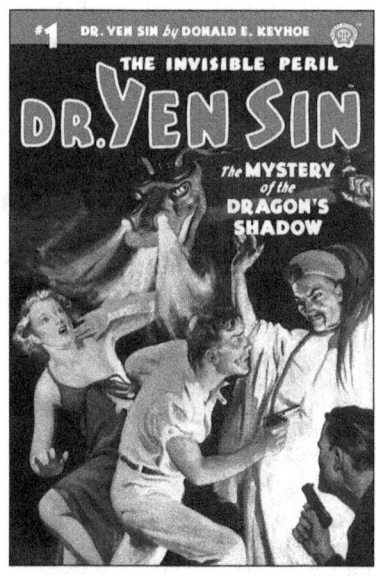
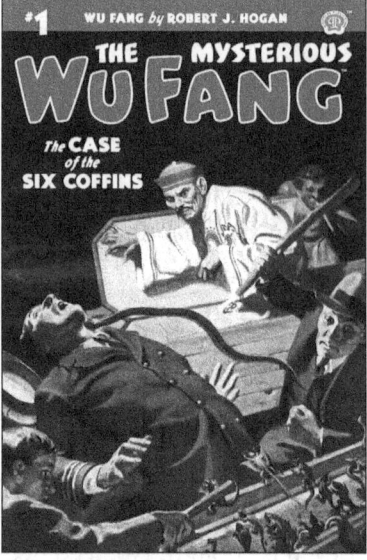